NAIL'S
CROSSING

NAIL'S CROSSING

KRIS LACKEY

A NOVEL

Printed in the United States of America

ISBN 978-1-4708-1407-6

1 3 5 7 9 10 8 6 4 2

CIP data for this book is available
from the Library of Congress

Blackstone Publishing
31 Mistletoe Rd.
Ashland, OR 97520

www.BlackstonePublishing.com

To my mother, Artene Hubbard
my wife, Karleene Smith
my daughter, Susan Lackey Parker

To Young Smith

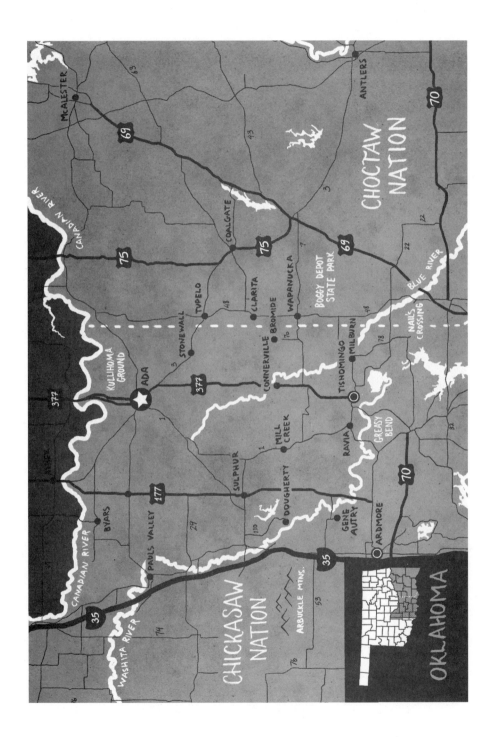

PROLOGUE

Hannah Bond had delivered a summons out on the rock prairie. She was heading back to the Johnston County Courthouse in Tishomingo, onetime capital of the Chickasaw Nation, when she passed a young woman standing beside a dusty red Chevy Aveo on the unshouldered margin of US 377. It was dusk, and the remote stretch of highway ran through a stark, boulder-strewn patch rare in Oklahoma. The fence junctions of stacked stone looked like something out of New—or old—England. The woman was staring at her cell phone. It was a dead zone, Bond knew. Most likely, the first rig to pass by would be a kindly rancher or roustabout who would change her tire and give her a goodbye salute, but …

Bond flicked on her strobes, made a U-turn, and pulled up in front of the car, which was headed south, same as she was. Hit by the headlights, the young woman squinted and frowned, let her arms fall at her sides. Clearly not looking for help from this quarter. Bond wasn't going to call in her temp plate or check her license, but the girl had no way of knowing this. And anyway, the deputy was accustomed to scaring people when she helped them. It never got any better when she unfolded all six feet two inches from the cruiser.

Not a big girl at all, this one. In the glare, her face looked pale against black hair that fell straight across her cheeks. A deep worry line creased her brow. Her lips were plump but a little drawn. Endurance, Bond guessed.

The left rear wheel was already jacked up, the doughnut spare and plastic hubcap lying on the ground. "Having some trouble?" Bond asked.

The young woman instantly relaxed. She swung her arm at the flat and dipped her knees. "I can't break the lugs. I stomped on the handle."

"Damn pneumatic wrenches. Go stand further in the bar ditch, away from the road."

In Bond's hands, the subcompact's jack handle and lug wrench looked like toys. She broke the lugs loose with no effort, affixed the spare, jacked the car down, and replaced all the equipment in the Aveo's trunk. Hand on the lid, she paused. "You got the keys with you?"

The girl jogged from the shadows, waving a long cigarette. "No. Wait, I don't! Oh, God, they're in the trunk! I never woulda thought of that." She yanked the keys from beneath a red suitcase and slammed the trunk lid. When she thanked Bond, she was facing away, staring up the dark road she had traveled.

By the time Bond made another U-turn, the Aveo's taillights had disappeared.

CHAPTER 1

Ever since he got back to Lighthorse Police headquarters at ten thirty, Bill Maytubby had been thinking about Mazen's chicken shawarma. He could just about smell the garlic. The egg whites he bolted at five a.m. had evaporated hours ago. He looked down at the clutter on his desk. He hated being in his office—in any office, really.

He could see the drought-seared Oklahoma hills behind downtown Ada, seat of Pontotoc County and modern capital of the Chickasaw Nation.

The clock next to a photo of the nation's governor read 11:58. Maytubby looked through the plate glass at the clock on the desk of his chief, Les Fox. It said 12:01. *Don't think about the grisly turkey buzzard*, he told himself. *Think about Jill Milton.*

And there she was, standing in Mazen's parking lot and smiling at Maytubby as he pulled up in the cruiser. At the end of Main behind her, the East Central University admin building shimmered like a mirage. There was too much white in the sky. The Citizens Bank thermometer flashed 105.

"Sergeant William of the Royal Lighthorse Police." She tapped the brim of his Mountie hat. "Sounds downright colonial."

"Change it to 'Maytubby.' Then it won't."

"Quite right, Sergeant. Carry on." She took his arm as they entered the restaurant. Normally, he braced for *the Chill*—that silent half second when he entered a public place in uniform and all eyes but the children's snapped down. Jill Milton rendered him invisible, though; everyone but the children stared at *her.*

Important wavy black hair to her shoulder blades, keen obsidian eyes, and a big, fierce smile. Maytubby also marked the diners' curiosity—tumblers turning in racial padlocks.

The waitress raised her eyebrows as they walked past. They nodded, and she went to tell the cook chicken shawarma, hummus. Jill said, "Sergeant, don't you have something on any of the tribal brass to make them rescind the panty-hose policy? It's the twenty-first century. It's been over a hundred degrees for a month!"

"Are you saying our government is co-opting the fashions of our oppressors?"

"No, I'm saying no guy would work for the nation if he had to wear a salmon polyester double-knit leisure suit."

Maytubby pointed to his campaign hat on the table. "We all have our burdens."

She snatched it up and put it on. The brim dropped to her nose.

"I'd say you're undermining my authority."

"I can't believe your people were my people's masters," she said.

The waitress appeared, and Maytubby put his finger to his lips and motioned her to give him his food and take Jill's away. He was twirling a hunk of shawarma on his fork when she lifted the hat.

"Hey!"

"Some of your people were masters, too."

Static crackled from his shoulder radio. He frowned and turned down the volume.

The waitress set Jill's hummus plate in front of her.

"Bill?" his shoulder said.

"Yeah, Sheila. What do we have?"

"Hello, Jill."

Jill Milton waved at the radio.

"OHP and nation road crew boss both called. Austin Love's silver-over-green jacked '78 F-one-hundred …" Maytubby grabbed his hat, smiled at his fiancée, looked longingly at the uneaten shawarma, and made for the door, "… east off One at Kullihoma Road. OHP abandoning pursuit on Fifteen-O-Five at the stomp grounds."

Maytubby pushed the black Lighthorse Charger over the breaks of the Muddy Boggy River, east of Ada, through Happyland toward the Kullihoma Grounds, where the nation gathered for ceremonial dances. He passed sun-scorched hay fields. A few skinny cattle stood around where ponds used to be. Ranchers had sold most of their herds in Ada weeks ago, when hay hit eighty dollars a big bale.

Leaving the highway, he faced a slalom course of construction signs and roadblocks on Kullihoma Road. A hundred yards of one-lane blacktop, a half mile of dirt, more one-lane blacktop. He blinked his lights at the Highway Patrol cruiser coming out. Jake Renaldo waved. Maytubby couldn't blame him for bugging out. Jake didn't know the roads in there. And in fresh pursuit, he couldn't arrest an Indian on tribal land. It was enough that he'd stay parked on Oklahoma 1 in case Austin Love came back west. Sheila would have a Pontotoc deputy where Kullihoma hit State 48 on the east side.

Luckily, the last couple of miles were paved on at least one side. He could make time without raising a giant dust cursor.

* * *

She had not gone gently, Majesty Tate. Her knuckles were bloody, and she had made the best of her gnawed fingernails, ripping sizable hunks of flesh from her killer. She had lost her silver Converse Chuck Taylors when she was dragged from her red Aveo, and her heels had torn the ground in every direction between there and her house. It looked as if a razorback or two had come through.

Finding the smeared antler-handle bowie had cost Maytubby the better part of a day. While FBI Evidence Response worked at

Tate's rented house—on a patch of tribal allotment land, which made it federal—he had walked miles of dusty road from Ms. Tate's house toward Witch Hole Lake on Delaware Creek, clear into the defunct resort of Bromide. On the left side coming down, on the right, back up into the hills. As he went, he tossed pebbles into the brush. When he flushed a swarm of blowflies, he walked to the dead thing—a coon, as it turned out. Near evening, he had found the knife in the bar ditch near Houghtubby Springs. A custom bowie. Whoever left it there either wanted it found or had a sorry arm.

*   *   *

Maytubby pulled into the stomp grounds, drove past the Thinking Warrior brush arbor and the Crazy Warrior arbor. It didn't take a skilled tracker to follow the pickup's trail. Love had fishtailed at every turn.

Even though Love had almost ten minutes on him, Maytubby drove slowly. He lowered his car windows, but closed them again when the cicada chorus washed in. Ears useless today. At each fork, the road got fainter—and rockier. It mattered less now that Maytubby knew Love veered left at every fork.

"Sheila?"

"Yeah, Bill."

"You get a Pontotoc deputy at Fifteen Thirty-Three and Forty-Eight?"

"Katz."

"Ask him to go south to Fifteen Fifty." Love was probably in Coal County by now.

Maytubby coddled the Charger down the ridge to Sincere Creek and jolted across its dry bed. He accelerated over a patch of chat, pinging bits of it up against the undercarriage, and gained the opposite bank with a little momentum. Rocks banged against the tranny and chassis. He was kicking up dust now. And he needed the four-by-four. Burr oak and sumac closed in on the track and scraped the cruiser's fenders. He could see where Love's pickup had snapped branches higher up. Before he crested the ridge, he was in deep shade.

When his grandmother was a child, she had seen the mischievous little people, the *konikosha*, here, and they had stolen her shoe. She had taught Maytubby to rearrange any place where he played, so the little people couldn't find their way to him. Those stories had given him the creeps.

He lowered the front windows. The trail switched back once. Braking for the hairpin, Maytubby instinctively scanned the road going up over his right shoulder. Then he looked again. Grass growing high in the ruts, no coat of dust on the oak leaves. Nothing in his mirror, nothing up the hill. He peered into the dark woods in front of him, let his gaze walk slowly to the left.

The hairs on his neck stood up, and he covered the grip of his Beretta. A Mississippi kite whistled as it rode the midday thermals, but the timber was still. Without taking his eyes off the thicket, he slapped the shifter into reverse so it would make a noise. A shadow twitched among the leaves, and when he refocused deeper in the blackjacks, Maytubby was staring into the slate-gray eyes of Austin Love. Greasy black hair plastered his handsome face and spilled over his bony shoulders. He grinned at Maytubby, fired the Ford's big eight, and roared onto the road behind the cruiser.

Dust and reefer smoke spun in the Charger's tonneau as Maytubby backed down the bluff, overcorrecting at every bend until the cruiser slewed hard and finally spun usefully around in a bootleg turn. He regained the creek just in time to see the pickup bouncing away down the rocky bed.

Love had no doubt planned for Maytubby to get halfway to Gerty before he did that. If he got to the Muddy Boggy that way, he would have to take out a few fences.

"Katz?"

"Yeah."

"Love's coming your way, down the Sincere."

"Driving down the *creek*?"

"'Fraid so."

"Phoo-*oo*!"

* * *

Renaldo was on the rusted truss bridge with Katz when Maytubby got out of the cruiser ten minutes later.

"This looks like a scene from *Deliverance*."

"My whole *life* looks like a scene from *Deliverance*," Renaldo said.

"Phoo-*oo*!" said Katz.

"See what I mean, Bill?"

"You hear his truck in there? Sounds like a sawmill?"

The others shook their heads. They stared down at the creek and listened in the silence between passing pickups towing cattle trailers to the Ada sale.

"Sheriff told me you found the knife," Renaldo said.

"Found *a* knife. FBI forensics might find out if it's *the* knife and if it has Love's prints on it."

Renaldo folded his arms and looked into the sky. "How do you know Love's prints are in the system?"

Katz and Maytubby snorted in unison.

"He wore that stag knife ever'where he went," Katz said, wiping the sweat off his hatchet face with his forearm.

"Where'd that girl come from?" Renaldo said. "What, Queen? Princess …?"

"Majesty. Tate. Albuquerque license address. Still haven't located next of kin. Nation rec ranger saw Love and her shooting eight ball at the Lazy K in Sulphur."

"How long's he been out of Mac?" Katz said.

"Twenty-six months. Gentlemen, I don't want to waste your time. Thank you."

* * *

Maytubby drove back to the stomp grounds entrance and parked under a concession arbor. Under the passenger seat, he found a small bottle of Ozarka water. Hot day. He took off his Smokey hat and tied on a blue bandanna. The warrant for Love's arrest, issued by the Chickasaw District court, crackled in his shirt pocket. Someone inside the court had alerted Love. Maytubby left his boots and socks on the floorboard, everything else but his cell phone and gun on the seat. If he disappeared, it would look downright Rapturish.

Until he picked up a deer trail into the back of the reservation, Maytubby scanned the stomp ground for glass shards. Jill mocked his awe of the Tarahumara runners. "It'll be all noble savage until you amputate a toe on a Choc beer bottle."

He found his pace and covered the two miles to Sincere Creek quickly. At the ford where he had lost Love, he stopped at the edge of the clearing, drank water, and listened. A distant crow, a semi testing the Sincere bridge. There would be no running down this creek, barefoot or shod. He picked his way along the rocky bed, wading a small pool here and there. The Ford's cartoon tires had overturned large rocks and spattered low limbs. A mile from the bridge, Maytubby climbed out of the creek and picked his way through the brush alongside.

Not a hundred yards on, he saw a big mess in the creek where Love had spun his tires trying to get a purchase on the steep bank. The pickup was nosed into a thicket. Maytubby pulled his Beretta and held it in both hands as he circled the truck, walking backward then forward. The driver's door was open—less racket in the woods. And by night, well, the dome light was smashed, likely during the Carter administration. He completed his circle and moved warily toward the pickup. He memorized the tires: forty-four-inch Ground Hawgs. Love's first few steps were clear—long smudges that suggested some haste. Maytubby was flattered. The cab was littered with Marlboro Red boxes and butts, nasty shirts, and jeans. A dark liquid had dripped and then dried on the floorboard and some of the clothes. He holstered the gun.

Love's first few steps led east, toward the bridge. But he knew there would be cops on the bridge—why he ditched the truck. Maytubby walked another circle, this one around the last smudge. A crushed blackjack acorn lay in a line with the other tracks. The next step left a clear print in deep sand. Herman Survivors—cheap at Walmart and common as dirt. After a rocky patch, a torn stem of poison ivy. He stopped looking for signs and followed the creek toward the bridge. In and around Majesty Tate's house, Survivor bootprints, many of them bloody.

Every fifty yards or so, the prints reappeared. They stopped at the fence where the State 48 right-of-way clearing began. Maytubby semicircled. Nothing. He went through the fence and up under the bridge, searching the shadow until his eyes adjusted. Hundreds of Survivor prints, crossing and recrossing. He shook his head. Love was waiting for them to get off the bridge. His exit trail led not back down to the river but around the abutment and up toward the road. Maytubby resisted a foolish impulse to climb to the road and have a look. The first driver who saw him would call the sheriff. He tried to remember whether a vehicle had crossed the bridge more than once when he and Renaldo and Katz were up there—maybe a friend Love had texted for a ride. Maytubby walked under the bridge and opened his cell phone. The tower on Potato Hill gave him a few bars. Possible. Was Renaldo's dash cam on?

He phoned Sheila as he left the road. Renaldo was writing up a speeder and would meet him in Stonewall.

"And, Sheila? I'm going to need mules."

CHAPTER 2

The aquamarine eyes of Aaron Coblentz lit on the horizon behind Hannah Bond. The wheels of his black buggy rocked back and forth as his buckskin gelding settled. He set the brake.

"Monday evening, this time? Hmm. You mean besides the speed demons from Wapanucka?"

"Yessir."

"They put glass packs on their mufflers. Spooks my horse."

"I bet."

"Monday … Monday I got a spoke mended at Miller's, bought cheese at the store in Clarita. Came back to Bromide on Limestone Road. Helped my wife can crookneck squash." Coblentz stared at the horizon while the buckskin's ears flicked off horseflies.

Several people had told Bond about the red Aveo and the jacked-up Ford, said the pickup had come and gone several times the week before. When she showed them a Photoshopped version of Love's truck, they all had said the same thing: "That's it."

She said again to Coblentz, "Did you see any unfamiliar vehicles on this road?"

"Don't remember any."

She showed him the doctored photo.

"Oh, *that*'n. I thought he was another speed demon from Wapanucka."

She showed him a red Aveo as well. "Yep, 'member that doodlebug, too."

Bond took a card from her pocket. "Do you have a phone shanty, Mr. Coblentz?"

"Phone in the barn," he said.

She handed him the card. "Call me if you remember any other vehicles."

He gave her a little salute, released the hand brake, and coaxed the gelding down the road. The orange reflective triangle on the buggy disappeared in the white dust.

Bond followed the road, passing Coblentz slowly, twisting up through dusty oaks and sycamores between some spring-fed pools. The road switched back at a crooked, overgrown hall-and-parlor house.

Two days earlier, after an anonymous call about a car door being left open too long, she had stepped past the red Aveo to the house's open front door and roused a bristling cloud of blowflies that drove her away before she could see what was in the shadowed interior. She batted them away from her face and snorted one out her nose. Folding a Sonic napkin from the cruiser over her face and brandishing a post oak branch, she rushed at the house, just to get it over with.

Before she gained the threshold, something inside fell. Bond dropped the branch, drew her stodgy revolver—Smith and Wesson Model 10—and duckwalked backward to the cruiser. Once behind it, she called for backup.

*   *   *

"Hannah. It's Maytubby. Four miles out. I know the house."

He was returning to Ada from a meeting at the Lighthorse substation in Thackerville. LHP and Johnston County officers were cross-deputized. Maytubby and Bond had trained together at

CLEET, the Council on Law Enforcement Education and Training.

Maytubby parked a hundred yards from the switchback, took his short-barrel binoculars from the cruiser, and walked into the woods. At the edge of the yard but still in shadow, he trained his glasses on the front doorway and waited for his pupils to adjust. Against the light of the room's double back window, a peaked silhouette bobbed spasmodically. The shadow looked like a child wearing a legionnaire's crested helmet.

When he was tucked behind Bond's cruiser, he showed her the field glasses and shrugged. "I don't think it's human," he whispered.

"Wall of flies. Reeks."

"Set?"

They split and crossed the yard quickly, guns out. At the edge of his vision, Maytubby saw the silver sneakers and the wild furrow leading to the door. He nodded at Bond to go first. A cloud of green flies billowed out the door, and Maytubby, squinting against the storm, banged his shoulder on the jamb. They halted and stared.

The thing stood on a chair, its outstretched wings filling the room. Gore hung from its beak. It fixed them with one gray-brown eye and hissed like a cat. A young woman's torso lay on the dining table. Her torn chin was visible at one edge. Her spindly legs, in filthy tight jeans, dangled off the edge.

Bond stared at the child legs for a few seconds, then frowned and raised her pistol.

"Don't do it, Hannah."

She sighted, closed her left eye. "You think I'll disturb *this* crime scene?"

"It's not ..."

"The nasty raping fucker," she snarled.

Maytubby looked at her. Her pistol wavered.

Slowly the wings descended and folded, and the bird hopped off the chair. Bond followed it with her pistol, and Maytubby holstered his and backed out of her line of fire. It lurched and rasped, kicking up magazines and cigarette butts with its absurd webbed feet. In the yard, its ascending wingbeats sounded like whiplashes.

Bond holstered her revolver but continued staring into the yard. "I know. Protected species. Discharged-weapon report."

Maytubby was silent.

"My sister was a protected species."

"Yes."

"And you see what walks out the door."

*   *   *

Crime-scene tape festooned the crooked house. She parked in the yard and stared into another hall-and-parlor house, in the Winding Stair Mountains, years ago. The Child Protective Services lady saying this was her and her sister's new foster home. Later, then, beyond the grinning face of her kneeling foster father, her sister's legs hanging stock-still from a kitchen table.

Maytubby had found the stag-handled knife. FBI Evidence Response wasn't even at the scene yet. He had just wandered off down the road. Said *nada.* After the agents had been there a while, they were pissed when he didn't come back. Then they were *really* pissed when he did come back. He had already found the knife.

Not until Bond learned that Love had been connected to Majesty Tate did that antler bowie that Maytubby found near the crooked house rattle into place.

Before Love was sent to Mac, she had arrested him in Pecan Bottom for thumping a young woman. He was amped and drunk, screamed at Bond when she kicked in the door, but then stood there swaying, leering at her with eyes the color of concrete. The girl gripped a chair back and held a bloody towel against her nose. "*Get that fucking cranker out of this house!*" Bond had wished he would go for the knife so she could shoot him. She had last seen it in a personal-effects tray in Tishomingo, when she booked him. The girl left the Johnston Memorial ER and skipped town. Love walked out the jailhouse door and took his bowie with him.

CHAPTER 3

Renaldo pointed to the OHP cruiser's little video screen. "That white Cobalt coupe, coming toward the camera. Dream catcher on the mirror. Male driver, no passengers. Elbows out—no AC. We seen that one before?"

Maytubby's video had been off when he was on the bridge. They were parked on the apron of a long-dead gas station on Old Oklahoma 3 outside Stonewall, a town named for a Confederate general. Maytubby's ancestors, he knew, had brought their African and Indian slaves with them in Removal. The Chickasaws sided with Jefferson Davis and were roundly punished for it.

"How would we know?" Maytubby said. "Half the cars down here are white Cobalts. I mean, I hope not."

Renaldo reversed the recording until a white 2004 Cobalt backed up fast toward the camera. Even at a distance, the dream catcher was visible against the front glass. He slowed the recording and paused it when the plate was clear.

On cardboard, in crude bold letters filled in with scribbles of blue ink: **LISENS LOST APPLY FOR**.

"Pay dirt," Maytubby said.

Renaldo wheezed a laugh.

"What's the dealer sticker?"

"Hmm. 'Bubba' is the first part. 'F-U-S-I-L-I-E-R.' Fusilier. Never heard of him."

"'*FUSE-lee-ay*'—it's a Cajun name. That dealership's in Jennings, Louisiana."

"Okay." Renaldo stared at him, smiled. "You say so." He called in the Cobalt to Troop F in Ardmore and Troop E in Durant. "What do you think Bubba's *real* first name is?"

"Your great-grandfather mined the Lehigh Seam. What was his first name?"

"How the hell do you know that?"

"Guy with an Italian surname from Coalgate? C'mon."

"Same as mine: Giacamo."

"So the great-grandsons of the French miners, some of them have the old names?"

"Like Emile Foushee?"

"Calls himself Butch?"

"Tiny."

"Which mine did Giacamo work?"

"Pinch Along."

"You think Love's ride made that lost-license tag to throw us off the scent?"

"'Lisens lost apply for'? No."

"Made it to throw someone else off the scent?"

"Somebody would've corrected his spelling."

"Not if that somebody was Love. He never finished fifth grade. The only hard word he can spell is 'pseudoephedrine.' Any stolen Cobalts matching?"

Renaldo typed a few words on his cruiser's laptop, shook his head, typed some more. "No. No recent transfers, either."

"We'll see what turns up. Thanks for your help, Jake." Maytubby got out of the cruiser.

Renaldo whistled the opening bars of "Dueling Banjos."

"Yeah, I know," Maytubby said.

He drove back up Oklahoma 48 until he passed Jaydee. Then he turned on his light bar and pulled onto the narrow shoulder. At every driveway and county road intersection, he got out of the cruiser and examined the right-of-way and culverts. The usual Coors cans and Walmart fliers, Chick-O-Stick wrappers, panties, feed sacks. Back in a thicket behind a fence, he saw a rusted half-buried refrigerator, painted with an ad for Hudson's Big Country Store in Coalgate. The immigrant Giacamo must have bought his dry goods there. A young Adam Richetti, later Pretty Boy Floyd's partner in crime, stuffed his pockets with some of the five thousand dimes flung one day each year from Hudson's roof.

Just shy of two miles outside Allen, in failing light, Maytubby saw a rectangle of cardboard torn from an Asics shoe box lying at the lip of a culvert, two loops of duct tape stuck on the logo. He parked on the grass to avoid disturbing any tread marks on the dirt drive over the culvert. Snapping on latex disposables, he slid through sunflowers and Johnson grass down into the bar ditch. Sure enough. He flipped the tag, hoping to find impressions of letters or numbers. But Duct-taper had a light touch. He considered slapping the tag over his Chickasaw Nation tag. Then he considered what the nation's governor would think if Maytubby passed him in Ada. He slipped the plate into a bag and threw it on the passenger seat. Then he took a small tape measure and a thin digital camera from his uniform pocket, laid a foot of metal tape across each tread mark, and photographed the marks. As he made his way back to Kullihoma Road, he radioed concerned parties.

The stomp grounds were lively. Floods from the GMC heavy wrecker backlit Love's jacked Ford as it was winched up. A single blue light on the FBI sedan strobed old Nub Jump as he unharnessed his pair of mules and coaxed them into a livestock trailer. Maytubby lowered his window for Chief Fox.

Fox leaned on the cruiser and stared at Jump. "We should sell peanuts," he said.

"How long's Nub worn that hat?"

Fox squinted. "Since I was a kid, all I know. Same ratty overalls, too. What kind of hat *is* that?"

"I believe that is a Cordobés. A Zorro hat."

"Like I said, we should sell peanuts."

"FBI get anything in the truck?"

"About fifty empty Marlboro packs. Dried blood on a door handle, floor, and seat. Prints, hair. Rock of something under the floor mat … That the plate won the spelling bee?"

Maytubby handed him the bag. "Could you ask the feds to dust this?"

"Why? So we can get the prints of one more dumb-ass twacker friend of Austin Love?"

"Stereotypes are so harmful. And you, a Native American."

Fox shook his head and took the bag. "Half. Same as Love."

* * *

Jill Milton watched Maytubby devour his cold shawarma from a take-out carton. At last, she said, "If we all ate as healthy as you, I'd be out of a job."

"That's about as likely as everybody suddenly losing the urge to gamble."

"Game."

"Game."

June bugs clattered against the lamplit windows of Jill's garage apartment.

"You ever see that mural of the little people in the old hospital?" she said.

"Sure."

"Some members wanted to move it to the new clinic. They had it cut out of the wall. Before they could move it, some other members said that was a bad idea because it would loose the wee folks to do mischief on the tribe. So the mural sits in its old room, in the dark."

He folded the last bite of pita bread, chewed a couple of times, and swallowed. "I never saw the little people. Now I'm too old—until the minutes before I die. My grandmother told me she did. You?"

"Who do you think taught me nutrition science? They used to teach some children natural medicine, but they keep up with the times."

"Got to," he said. "Or they end up in the lore bin."

"Sol Stoddard was back. In Paoli, for God's sake."

"What kind of audience could he get? I mean, who in Paoli would object to a children's play promoting good nutrition?"

A snare roll of cicadas rose in the hot night.

"He had a claque. People with signs."

"Like 'Diabetes is good for our children'?"

"Try 'Nanny state brainwashing our children.' Stoddard also claims the animal characters deliver a veiled assault on hunting and meat eating. And the Eagle Play, because it's connected to the CDC, is part of a liberal conspiracy to destroy the 'Oklahoma way of life,' as he calls it."

"Any cameras?"

"Just KXII in Ardmore. Nobody from the city." She broke eye contact for an instant. "There was this guy—aviators, ball cap visor pulled down, red hair. Wore a T-shirt that said 'Tolerance is the virtue of a man without convictions.' 'Tolerance' in big orange caps with flames rising from the letters. He was yelling"—she shook her fist in the air—"'The Eagle Play promotes spiritual *relativism*!'"

"I thought you were going to say 'barbarous Chickasaw rites.'"

"Stoddard's going to need Chickasaw votes someday."

"He hopes. His former district was a hundred miles north. Not doing himself any favors around here."

Jill Milton nodded, scowling. "Yeah … Well, Brother Tolerance? When I was coming out of the school, he broke away from the posse and stood between me and the parking lot."

Maytubby lowered his chin a little.

"I stopped, and he walked into my personal space. Then he turned his head away from me and stage-whispered in this weird accent, 'Brainwashin' our children is bad enough. But you don't hardly look Indian. We don't need no outsiders.' He turned his head so I could see my face in his glasses, and then leaned just enough toward me so I didn't have to tilt my head back. He said, 'Y'heard me?' Then he backed away a few steps before he turned and walked away."

The last of the cicadas outside fell silent.

Maytubby's lips tightened. "That's crossing a big line, Jill. You think this was just another mouthy prick, or somebody who could be an actual danger to you?"

"I don't know."

"So why don't I ask Fox to assign a Lighthorse escort for you and the Eagle crew?"

"Not now. It would spook the school administrators, and nobody needs that."

Maytubby paced the apartment for almost a minute, then washed his fork and put it in the drainer. Jill Milton stood beside him at the sink, and they stared out the garage apartment's window, at the field of sodium lights spreading away from the King's Road bluff toward Ahloso. Her tiny window unit labored against the evening heat.

"Tell me you didn't track Austin Love in your bare feet."

"Okay."

She pursed her lips. "He's a major thug?"

"Went to Mac for second-conviction meth possession with intent. Half-dozen misdemeanor battery convictions on his sheet."

"No weapons?"

Maytubby shook his head.

"So he's a *middling* thug."

"Depends. Hannah Bond arrested him in Tish once for pounding a woman. Woman skipped."

"Oh. Considering what happened to her baby sister, I'm surprised Hannah didn't just haul him out in the Twelvemile Prairie and shoot him."

"Somebody better find him before she does."

She touched his forearm. "Can you see that beautiful valley, or do you only see a landscape of violent memories?"

"When I'm with you, all I see is the beautiful valley."

"Good."

CHAPTER 4

Bond liked to park her cruiser where Blue River crosses Oklahoma 7 on a long straightaway near the Deadman Springs Road intersection. Sitting there in the shade of a sycamore, she could clock what vehicles came by, and otherwise just watch the clear river spill over a limestone shelf. In a land of sluggish red-mud rivers, the idyllic Blue stuck with you.

She had stopped the only white Cobalt. It was owned by its driver, a redheaded pastor from Tushka whose eyes were a little too far apart. He handed Bond a tract before he drove away. It had a crude drawing of a glowering red devil on the front, above the caption "satan is waitin'." She crumpled it up and stuffed it in the ashtray. He hadn't waited for *her.*

The next car that passed in the same direction was doing eight over. Not excessive, but the driver was on his cell and didn't slow when he passed her. She scooted off the grass, lit up her strobes, and followed the white Lexus ES, pretty far back, for half a mile. Normally, she would have turned on her siren, but she was curious to see where he was going. From time to time, he took his free hand off the wheel and hammered the air.

When the Lexus crossed into Atoka County, Bond switched off

her strobes and fell back a little more to see where the angry man was going. Then she saw the Cobalt a half mile ahead. The angry man slowed. He also put down his phone and stopped waving. When the Cobalt turned right on Park Road, toward Boggy Depot State Park, the Lexus followed. Bond didn't. The angry man might be oblivious, but the preacher had been tipped.

The next road south, Wards Chapel, would take her to Boggy Depot Road—quickly, if she broke the law. In four minutes, she struck the ghost town. Saw no cars, only a weed-choked cemetery and a few stone foundations. Maytubby had told her that his ancestors, and his fiancée's, had survived smallpox in a Removal camp here.

Bond turned north and pulled into the park's south entrance, waving at the attendant. Like other cash-strapped state facilities in the region, the park was now operated by the Chickasaw and Choctaw nations. She parked behind some junipers and walked the perimeter in thick brush until she saw the Cobalt idling in a secluded campsite. The park was otherwise deserted. Within a minute, the white Lexus pulled in behind the Cobalt. The angry man got out of the Lexus and sat in the Cobalt's passenger seat.

Bond shrugged and walked back toward the cruiser. Just another parson on the down-low, hooking up with some city guy he met. Wouldn't make trouble in Tushka. Satan is waitin'? Maybe. She returned to the sycamore on the Blue, ticketed a gas-patch roustabout and one of the Wapanucka speed demons who so riled Aaron Coblentz.

The hills behind Bromide rose a little above the prairie. Love had almost certainly fled east, into the rough country of Pushmataha—the Ouachitas. But she squirmed at the thought that he might be hiding under her nose.

Without radioing Tish, she pulled onto 7 and headed west toward some isolated reaches of Tar Branch, above Lake Texoma. The gummy asphalt sizzled under her tires. Dust devils buffeted the little islands of sumac and spun up the topsoil a half mile into the sky.

She knew which houses the state narcs were watching for meth doings, and avoided them, choosing instead houses with a better view of them than the crankers had of their neighbors. The first was a time-stained mobile home that once, maybe in the sixties, had been a beige and brown two-tone but was now the color of black mold. It had vomited out rotted furniture, spavined toys, rusted corn cobbers, animal bones. Two matted mongrels lunged at the cruiser, straightening their log-chain tethers. One of them got his teeth under a fender. Bond could hear metal popping. She backed up out of reach, then got out and stood in the yard.

A curtain snapped open, then shut. Bond waited. The dogs writhed. Ten minutes. Twenty minutes. Sweat coursed down her neck and back. She stood stolidly, fingering the folded mug shot of Austin Love in her palm. She didn't show paper. People feared cops, but they feared cops with paper more.

Bond's shadow had visibly moved before the door flew open and a thin woman in a yellow BEAVERS BEND wifebeater stepped down onto the single cinder block that served as the front step. The dogs barked maniacally. She had butterfly and dragon tattoos on her chest and arms. She stood with her hands on her hips. A pencil line of tobacco juice rode the crease of her lips.

"What do you wawnt?" she shouted over the dogs.

"Good afternoon, ma'am. I'd like to show you a picture of a man and ask if you've seen him around here." Bond now unfolded the eight-by-ten enlargement and held it toward the woman. She tried to see what the woman's eyes would do before she spoke, but she was too far away.

The woman whirled back into the doorway and shouted over her shoulder, "I ain't seen *nobody.*" She slammed the door.

Who could blame her.

Backtracking to avoid driving in front of the meth house, Bond drove four miles to get three hundred yards. She looked for a name on the freshly painted mailbox but found only the absurd street number, 148625 North Dove Road, that had replaced a simple rural route number. She followed a long driveway paved with discarded asphalt shingles laid in perfect rows like a roof. It ended before a neat blond brick ranch with green cast-iron porch posts. Three holly shrubs grew on either side of the porch, each trimmed into a strangely perfect sphere.

Bond rang the doorbell, which played the opening notes of "Für Elise." A middle-aged woman with a silver bob opened the door, smiled uneasily, and said, "Good afternoon, Officer. Please come in." Bond followed her down a short hallway, wondering at her starched lace collar, wool skirt, and white pumps. An outfit like that, she hadn't seen since she was young—and even then only on elderly ladies. The house smelled like camphor and tapioca.

In the living room, the woman directed her to a blue satin couch with crocheted doilies on the armrests. "Can I get you some tea?"

She means hot tea. Bond stared at a crystal bowl filled with dinner mints. She had never been offered hot tea in her life. It was 107 degrees outside. "No, thank you, ma'am. I'm fine."

The woman sat in a blue satin wing chair and folded her hands in her lap. "What can I do for you, Officer?"

Bond unfolded the mug shot of Austin Love and held it out. "Have you ever seen this man?"

The woman's hazel eyes flared, not with recognition but with anger.

"Do you recognize this man?"

"What has he done?"

"Have you seen this man?"

"Oh. I apologize. No, Officer. And if I had, I wouldn't forget it. Those black teeth! That horrible … leer."

Bond folded and pocketed the mug shot. "His name is Austin Love. He's a murder suspect. As far as we know, he's not in this area." She handed the woman her card. "If you do see him, please give me a call. And your name, if you don't mind?"

"Evelyn Hunter." She opened a drawer on the end table next to her chair and slipped the card inside. "And, Deputy Bond," she said, reaching farther back into the drawer, "if I do call you …" She pulled out a Smith and Wesson Wonder Nine and laid it on the table. "… it will be to report that I have shot this man on my property."

Bond stood. "Please call the sheriff's office. Love is only a suspect."

Evelyn Hunter stood as well. "This county covers over six hundred square miles. At any given time, how close is the nearest deputy to this house?"

Bond looked at her, said nothing.

"You're at my house because it's the closest to that clutch of maggots in the bottom."

Again Bond didn't reply.

"So," Evelyn Hunter said, as she nodded toward the hall.

"So," Bond said.

CHAPTER 5

At 5:00 a.m., Maytubby read everything the FBI had learned about Majesty Tate, and then faxed Love's mug and Tate's driver's license photo to all seven Chickasaw convenience stores. He was standing at the entrance to the nation's Family Life Center at six, waiting for the manager to open up. He set his gym bag down and checked his watch: 6:12. A grasshopper landed on his wrist. The drought was driving them onto irrigated land. In Nuevo Laredo, he had once eaten a whole bag of them. They tasted like chili-fried straw.

By the time the manager opened up, it was too late for Maytubby to lift. He dressed out for a run, all but the shoes. Running barefoot along Broadway or around the Ada airport had got him a couple of ugly cuts and too many goatheads to count, and, of course, it provoked no end of eye rolling and snorts from Jill Milton. So he had located the woman who owned the undeveloped land between the gym and the Canadian River, and got permission to run its cow paths. Now he began and ended each run ducking between strands of barbed wire.

The FBI had not yet located Tate's next of kin—the parents listed on the California birth certificate she had used to get her

New Mexico license. She would have turned twenty-six the day after she was killed. She had spent six months in a foster home when she was eight. At seventeen, she had been arrested for soliciting in Amarillo, Texas. The charge had been dismissed, and her record was otherwise clean.

Her GoPhone listed no contacts and had no record of messages. She had called two other prepaid phones, neither matching an owner and neither still active, and two Oklahoma City motel rooms. One was at the Western Sky, the other at the Old Route 66 Motel. Both 1940s vintage motels were well maintained, red brick with white trim, and both had neon signs featuring a green saguaro cactus, never mind that the closest real saguaro was three states and a thousand miles away. None of the day clerks at either place recognized her photograph. Maytubby Googled the motels.

She had never, under the name Majesty Tate, had a cell phone contract. On one crumpled pink slip of paper, she had written Love's number, the number of the pro shop at the Oklahoma City Country Club in Nichols Hills, and the club's address on Grand Boulevard. None of the clerks or caddies or regulars there when the agent visited recognized her photograph.

An ink pen in her purse was from the Oklahoma History Center, a museum near the state capitol. She had bought the Aveo used from a dealership in Guthrie. The salesman recognized her face and recalled only that she had paid cash, mostly fifties, and that she had exact change, down to the penny. The address on the bill of sale, Maytubby found for himself, was a boarded-up duplex in a decaying precinct of north Oklahoma City. Two weeks before she was murdered, she had moved into the Bromide house, on an old Chickasaw allotment, and paid its owner two months' rent, again in fifty-dollar bills.

Maytubby ran the little bluff above Canadian Sandy Creek, dodging cow flops and goathead runners. Scissortails and mourning doves flew between dusty oak groves, and down at the bottom he surprised a whitetail buck. It took the opposite bluff in two bounds and was gone.

Majesty Tate clearly drifted with the running underclass. Whereas most drifted west or in circles, she had drifted east. The medical examiner would tell him if she had been using. If so, her connection to Austin Love would be clearer. She paid cash for everything, she used disposable phones, and she called motel rooms. She might have been dealing. Or hooking. Or both. Maytubby noticed that the path he was running had worn a rut into the Permian red bed. A little allegory, he thought, warning him to stop making glib connections between Tate and Love.

What did the motels have in common? They weren't chains, they were well enough maintained to get AAA endorsements, they were not on interstate highways, they were survivals not revivals, and they both probably owed their survival to nostalgia tourists following the old path of the mother road. They were both on lots that bordered older, respectable neighborhoods. He imagined a beeline between the state capitol and the Oklahoma City Country Club. It nearly struck both motels. Guthrie was thirty miles from the other places. The only connection Maytubby saw: it was the old territorial capital. Sometimes the junk in his head got in the way.

Bromide was more than a hundred miles south of all the other places, which were above the North Canadian. A long-dead town, almost a century removed from its heyday as a trendy resort. Maytubby recalled that it was founded by the headmaster of Wapanucka Academy, a Chickasaw girls' school. Bindweed shrouded the derelict walls of Bromide's four hotels. It was located at the end of a state highway with a letter after its number—a letter a ways down the alphabet. And the town's back was against the hills. The house Tate had chosen was up in those hills.

If she had been running from someone, which she probably always was, she hadn't run very far from the previous scenes of her life. This was nothing new. People preferred the devil they knew in the next county to the devil they didn't in Memphis. It seemed Majesty Tate had overlooked the devil in between.

On a rise, Maytubby jogged to a stop, put his hands on his hips. *The creep who threatened Jill. Who is he?*

He looked down on the Canadian's broad floodplain. A river so young it hadn't even made a dent. The white trunks of cottonwoods blazed against the red river sand. A rafter of wild turkeys foraged among them. Feasting on grasshoppers, Maytubby conjectured.

He turned and retraced his route, making a mental list of Love's pre-Mac buddies as he loped along. He could remember where some of them lived back then. Most were probably gone or dead. Love's sister, Patty, used to live outside Sulphur with a vile man named Raleigh Creech. One of Love's uncles lived in Mill Creek, Johnston County.

A junked refrigerator that seemed to be sledding down a cascade of trash in a wash behind the landowner's house reminded Maytubby of Love's Coalgate connection. What was that guy's name? Fox face, widow's peak, long ears, red hair, pointy nose. Always slinking, there but not there. Contracted with oil-and-gas companies to cut weeds around the wellheads. Wiley—that was it. Maytubby smiled at the mnemonic. Wiley Bates.

Of course, Austin Love might be holed up way east, in the Jack Fork Mountains. Unless they were his Memphis.

Maytubby showered, dressed, and searched *Oklahoman* obits on his cruiser's computer. He found two of Love's old renegade cohort among the dead—no surprise—but not his sister or uncle. Raleigh Creech and Wiley Bates were still among the quick. The slow quick. That left just two petty recidivists he could scout before he officially went on the clock. He called Hannah Bond on his cell. She was at the Downtown Diner on Capitol Street in Tishomingo, two blocks from the old Chickasaw capitol.

"Hey, Bill."

"What's for breakfast?"

"Your girlfriend's a dietitian, right?"

"Yeah."

"I ain't sayin'."

"We've been through too much together."

"Still ain't sayin'."

He told her everything he had learned about Majesty Tate.

"Confusing," she said.

"If you're up around Mill Creek this morning, could you talk to Love's uncle? Lives on Sykes Road, on Bee Branch. Name's Carter Love. Green cottage with a chicken coop in the side yard. And see if he knows where Patty lives."

"I have to serve a subpoena in Troy. Extra five miles, easy."

"He's a speaker. You can try out your Chickasaw pleasantries."

As Maytubby neared Stratford, orchards of withered peach trees appeared to his left and right. The usual peck baskets lining the stand shelves had shrunk to gallon baskets, and the fruit was small and mottled. Just beyond the town, he turned south on a numbered dirt road and followed it until he found the little red-brick ranch house he remembered from years ago. The automobile carcasses perched on blocks in the yard were exactly the same except for the oak saplings growing out of the trunks and floorboards.

A once-blonde woman of forty or so opened the door and stared through the screen with sleep-addled eyes. She wore a long, tattered Sooners T-shirt as a nightgown. Crossed her arms over her chest and didn't move to open the screen. Maytubby didn't recognize her. "Good morning, ma'am. Is Donnie Frederick at home?"

She stared at him. "Which home you mean?" She was awake now. "He always had several, I learned. Drywall job in Sherman, he said. Hayin' in Marietta, he said."

She made a moue and raised an eyebrow. He waited for her to continue.

"Followin' the harvest, he said. Huh! Followin' his pecker, more like." She looked to the side and smiled faintly. "He musta took his eye off even that sometime or other, and lost it." She looked Maytubby in the eye again and started to laugh. "You can't imagine a man not knowin' where his pecker's at ... Oh, I forgot. You know Donnie."

Maytubby smiled.

She opened the screen. "Officer, you want a cup of coffee? Fresh. Cain's."

"Sounds good, thanks, but I have to go serve and protect."

"I th'ew Donnie out more'n a year ago. Out of his own house. I been payin' the note two years. He was a priceless turd."

"Do ..."

"I got no idea. Believe me, I'd tell you if I knew."

Maytubby unfolded a photo of Austin Love and held it out. "Have you ever seen this man? He used to run with Donnie."

She took the photo and brought it close to her face, making a show of being helpful. "Let me think ..." She looked into the sky, as if Love might be floating there. She tapped her chin.

Maytubby was impatient to get on to his next rascal. He reached for the photo, and she lifted it out of his reach. "I just might of seen this guy over at Ardmore yersty. I think I did. At a stoplight." She handed the photo back to him.

Maytubby didn't believe her. "Do you remember the make, model, or color of the vehicle?"

She gave him the stink-eye. "I thought you were asking my help." She closed the screen.

"And I am."

"You thought I was lyin'."

"If you can recall anything about the vehicle, it would help."

"Well, I can. It was a old gray pickup."

Maytubby took an index card with his grocery list on it and pretended to write down what she had said. "That's good. Thanks."

The door slammed behind him.

On his way to Wanette, Maytubby reluctantly spread the fib about Love in the old gray pickup way south in Ardmore. There were reasons not to. Officers in the east might pay less attention. Everyone driving such a rig down south would draw the cop stare.

As he waited at an intersection for the cross traffic to pass, a 1966 Ford pickup, gray primer stem to stern, rolled to a stop beside him. "For instance," Maytubby hissed at himself.

He fought the urge to look into the cab. He looked into the cab. Love was not there. The driver, though. His pale head faced straight forward, a nest of Johnny Rotten copper hair on top, but his left eye was just a click too far over. Maytubby started when he realized the eye was regarding him. He quickly looked up the road in the opposite direction.

CHAPTER 6

In the rearview mirror of Hannah Bond's cruiser, the old Chickasaw Nation Capitol, built of local Pennington granite, commanded the hill above the Johnston County Courthouse. It was a stately thing, with its silver cupola and snapping pennant. It buoyed her when she left town, and greeted her when she returned. A public work that was lasting and grand. The new courthouse looked like a tire store.

State 22 threaded some small granite outcrops and crossed the little canyon dug by Pennington Creek. Bond turned north on State 1 and followed the Burlington Northern Santa Fe tracks through stands of gnarled red cedars. Rail sidings wandered off toward industrial sand-and-gravel pits hidden by the trees. The shoulder grass was dead.

She made short work of the subpoena. She hadn't told the dispatcher or the sheriff about Carter Love. She was supposed to be taking donations from the speed demons of Wapanucka. Maytubby's directions were exactly enough, as always. Just after Sykes Road crossed Bee Branch on a little plank bridge, Carter Love's green cottage appeared on the right. A row of spindly bois d'arc trees broke the south wind. A little elevated coop of rabbit wire and plywood scraps held some Iowa blues, which fretted when Bond walked across the yard.

Carter Love opened the door before she knocked. He was shorter than the deputy, well made, with a dense thatch of silvering hair. The nephew's strong facial structure was softened in the uncle.

"*Chokma?*" Bond said in her best night-class Chickasaw. She didn't make eye contact. Maytubby had told her how hard it was for him to unlearn this habit of respect.

"*Hohmi. Ishnako?*" Love smiled faintly.

"*Hohmi. Anchokma akinnih. Yakoke.* Deputy Bond *Sa holhchifoat.*"

"It's hot already," Love said. "Would you like a glass of tea?"

"Yes, thank you," Bond said.

"Have a seat, Deputy."

Love set a sweating blue metal tumbler in front of Bond and then sat down in a cowhide chair with horn armrests. The shade on the lamp beside his chair was printed with cattle brands.

"You a cattleman, Mr. Love?" She nodded at the lampshade.

He turned in his chair and craned his neck to see where she was pointing. After studying the shade a few seconds, he turned back to Bond. "I never looked at that lamp before. Huh. That ... and this"—he pointed at the chair with his thumb—"came to me when my father passed away. No, I retired last year from the federal government. Forty-two years at the park in Sulphur—Platt National when I started, Chickasaw Recreation Area now. All the creeks in there are dry this summer."

Bond nodded, listened to the hens clucking. "Mr. Love, I'm working on a case with the Lighthorse."

"Which man?"

"Sergeant Maytubby.

"William?"

"Yes."

"I talked to him at the Nation Festival in Tishomingo year

before last. A gentle boy. Quick. Both ways. I knew his *inki'*."

Bond couldn't read what Love thought about the father.

"Mr. Love, Sergeant Maytubby and I need to talk to …"

Love began to nod.

"… your nephew Austin."

Love watched her mildly. "Austin has enlarged my circle of friends in law enforcement."

Bond smiled.

"I already knew the skins."

She laughed.

"Austin's *ishki* passed, or you would be talking to her." He paused. "This is not about that young woman in Bromide."

"Yes."

Love trained his eyes on the wall beside Bond's head. "He's not here, Deputy. I haven't seen him. I don't know where he is. My friends in law enforcement always know more about his buddies and his doings than I do."

"His sister Patty?"

Love shook his head. "Last I knew, she was still with that bum Creech."

Bond finished her tea and stood up. Love kept his seat and looked up at her.

"Thanks for your time, Mr. Love. And the tea."

"What I said about Austin is true. But so is this: he *was* here."

Hannah Bond sat back down.

"The night that girl was killed—if she was killed at night. I saw his dinosaur tracks in my yard. I saw the fuel gauge in my pickup. Saw where he wiped his handprints off the filler cap. And he didn't leave a siphon hose lying around."

"He ever done that before?"

"No."

Has he visited you or anyone in your family since he was released from prison?"

"Not me. Nobody else I know of."

"Do you mind if I photograph the tread marks?"

"No."

Bond stood again. This time, Love rose with her. "*Yakoke.*"

He nodded.

Until she got the Bromide turnoff behind her, Bond couldn't think about calling Maytubby. Only when she pulled the cruiser under her accustomed sycamore on the Blue could she relax.

Maytubby answered. "Pork sausage and biscuits and pepper gravy."

"I still ain't sayin'."

"You're a hard woman, Hannah Bond."

"I interviewed Carter Love."

"How was your Chickasaw?" "I ain't sayin'."

"What did you learn?"

"Austin paid his uncle's truck a visit the night we think Tate was killed. Siphoned off most of a tank."

"Carter's old heap, Austin'll be driving with rusty gas. Might make him easier to catch. Uncle see him do it?"

"No. Huge-ass tire prints in the sand. I'll send you photos. Came from the east, left to the east."

"Back to State One. No rain in months, so no mud prints to follow."

"So Austin was either broke or didn't want to be seen at a gas station—or both.

"Or it was just late at night and he knew where to get free gas. Buffalo omelet with a cornbread muffin?"

"You got to start eatin', man."

CHAPTER 7

The rusted camelback trusses of the Canadian bridge, looming above burr oaks and sycamores, weren't going to restore his runner's high. Maytubby had always felt superstitious when he snaked through the shadowy bosk on the narrow approach to the bridge, as if the present and its citizens were being erased behind him. It wasn't only that the onetime railroad bridge was old, a relic of a time just before statehood, when the federal government had almost completed its demolition of the Chickasaw Nation. More that it was the only visible man-made thing, and it was really long and tall and skinny—a Gothic cage worthy of Tim Burton.

The opposite approach was blind, the bridge one lane, so Maytubby switched on his strobes. Once he was across, in the Citizen Potawatomie Nation, he turned them off and sped over a little rise toward Wanette. A BIA commission freed him to move across Indian national borders.

Sully Wolf and Austin Love, Maytubby knew, had shared a cell more than once before Love waded deep into meth. People said they broke enough cues in southeast Oklahoma to let the owner of Ada Billiards Supply retire early. But they hadn't made any friends among the small-town docs summoned in the wee hours to stitch up their victims' scalp wounds.

Maytubby had heard conflicting Wolf sequels. Ol' Sully went straight, runs a little construction bidness out of his pickup—salt of the earth now. Ol' Sully took the straight and narrow for a spell, then backslid, then reformed again. He had inherited his mother's territorial house, built on a Potawatomie allotment between Wanette and Asher. Maytubby saw the dogtrot cabin, a breezeway down its middle, through a grove of pecans planted long ago. It hadn't seen a paintbrush in living memory. Wolf had replaced a few planks, and the fresh wood gleamed yellow. His woodpile for the coming winter was already eight feet high in the middle. A pickup—an old, gray pickup, Maytubby grimly noted—was parked across the dogtrot's gap. Shaky block letters on the door spelled out "WOLF CARP."

There was a plausible front door on each side of the dogtrot, so Maytubby knocked on both. From the hearth side, he heard some commotion. A deep voice shouted, "Minute!"

Soon, a wooden peg traveled up a groove in the door, and Maytubby gaped at it. When the door opened, Wolf's frame filled the whole space. His little green bloodshot eyes spun freckles across his cheeks and down into his Teddy Roosevelt mustache. The 'stache softened his aspect and rendered his once-feral eyes almost kindly.

"You have a wooden latch," Maytubby said.

Wolf looked at the peg in the groove a full three seconds. Then he looked down at Maytubby out of the corner of his eye and said drolly, "I didn't steal it, and if I remember right, I didn't whack anybody with it. You gonna arrest me for possession?"

Maytubby was about to say he had never seen a wooden latch that wasn't on a gate or in a museum. "You've kept the house intact," he said.

Wolf continued to stare at the latch for some time before he looked at Maytubby again. "I don't like to bring my work home," he said. Maytubby thought he was joking, but waited for a sign before he laughed. Wolf finally smiled.

Maytubby tried a yes-or-no question: "You seen Austin since he got out of Mac?"

It didn't work. Wolf now stared out over the pecan grove like a ship's captain surveying the cold North Atlantic from his pilot-house. A mockingbird began to pitch a fit.

"What's he done?"

"I need to talk to him. There was a murder down by Tishomingo. Young woman."

The South Canadian now became the object of Wolf's contemplation. Maytubby furtively checked his watch. The earth turned on its axis.

"Huh," Wolf said.

Talking to anyone else, Maytubby would have thought petit mal.

"He started pushin' that whiz, he got mean." He saw Maytubby looking at him. "-er."

"Have you seen him, Sully?"

Wolf folded his arms across his chest. That was a yes. But where? Maytubby watched the little eyes to see where he was looking. South and not east. Most of a minute passed. To the west, an AWACS C5-A descended for its final to Tinker AFB.

"He ain't been *here*."

"You stopped running with him a long time ago."

"You got that right."

Maytubby worked that vein. "He went down pretty fast."

Wolf rubbed the stubble on his chin, then pinched the bridge of his nose. "Did."

A hot breeze ruffled native elm volunteers clumped around the yard. "Murdered a girl, you say?"

"Looks that way."

"Huh." Wolf shook his head, stubbed his boot on the porch planks. "Bad."

"Bad."

Wolf walked to the edge of the porch and exhaled loudly, as

if to clear his throat of all moral obstructions. "I finished a job in Stonewall yesterday evenin'. Had a few at Hoyt's out on old Three toward Tupelo. I was takin' a piss and saw him out the back window. He was in the passenger seat of a old Dodge pickup—kind with the google eyes. Gray. Talkin' to the driver and another guy standin' in the lot. I didn't reconize any of 'em. None of 'em come inside. They all left. Guy standin' left in a little white car."

Wolf didn't look too pleased with himself. He did not want to pick the vehicles out of a lineup on the LHP cruiser's computer. It made his snitching too real. But he did. The pickup was a 1966 Dodge D100. The white sedan, Maytubby didn't need to be told: a 2004 Cobalt.

Wolf got out of the cruiser. It was the first thing he had done quickly. He stalked toward his house. Through the window of the cruiser, Maytubby said, "You think he would hang with Bates or Creech?"

Wolf pointedly shrugged his massive shoulders. He went in the house, slammed the door, and dropped its wooden latch.

* * *

By the time Maytubby pulled into the parking lot of the Johnston Education Building in Ada, he had radioed everyone who needed to know that Love had been seen in the gray Dodge pickup in Stonewall. Chief Fox understood that his investigator would be in the field all day.

As he was now, watching Jill Milton's car turn onto Ninth Street. Her fierce smile cut the air a block away. He frowned severely, made the *Halt!* gesture, and motioned her into a parking space.

"Officer, what have I done?"

"You don't know. Yet another reason you shouldn't be on the road."

"Where should I be?" she said, getting out of her car.

"Forging the ideals of our nation?"

"How about canning the chow-chow of our nation?"

A hot wind carried the scent of Johnson grass. American and Chickasaw Nation flags whipped on a metal standard, their snaps pinging.

"Ah, the demonstration kitchen. We eat what we can, and what we can't, we can."

"We're taping for Chickasaw TV today."

"Woo. You been practicing your flashy canning moves, Doctor?"

"Unceasingly."

"Just so you keep things in perspective. Canning is not the only thing in life."

"That's what you said about low-salt cooking."

"Funny, the woman I had lunch with at Mazen's—not noted for its low-sodium menu—looked a lot like you."

"Will she be there today?"

Maytubby took her forearm in his palm and rubbed it with his thumb. "Sorry, Jill. This morning, one of Austin Love's old pack told me he saw Love in Stonewall last night."

"Is that what they call a hot tip?"

"Not for the last forty years."

"Are you going to tighten the noose?"

"If this is 1965."

"What *do* you say?"

"Somebody told us where the suspect was, and now we're going to see if we can find him somewhere around there."

"You would have been a lot sexier in 1965."

"So would you. Panty hose were scarce."

She smiled and looked away, gnawed her thumbnail. "People got your back somewhere around there?"

"Yes ma'am."

"Hannah Bond?"

"Not unless Love's gone into Johnston County."

"Jake Renaldo?"

"If OHP has put him somewhere around there. I've got Lighthorse and Pontotoc County cops and state police."

"Like what's-his-name, the Goober."

"Katz."

"Reassuring."

"Katz is okay. Self-awareness is not essential in law enforcement. In fact …" He bent over and looked in the cruiser's side-view mirror, ran his hand through his thick black hair.

She bit her lip and kicked him, side of the foot, seat of his britches.

They laughed and grabbed each other's hands. She gave him a look that told him to be careful.

"I will," he said.

They turned away from each other. As Maytubby opened his cruiser's door, she said, "Hey!" and pointed down Ninth Street. "I've seen that car somewhere."

He followed her hand and saw a new white Lexus ES accelerating west. Waxed and new, it stood out in Ada. They watched it disappear.

"Call me if you remember where."

"I will."

CHAPTER 8

The twists and narrow bridges of Old Oklahoma 3 spoiled Maytubby's time to Coalgate, but it had to be—Austin Love had already shown that he preferred the old road's scrubby camouflage and easy escape routes to the high, sunny, well-mown new version. As leaning bollard stumps snapped past his window, Maytubby fought the impulse to take this or that road trailing up a shaggy hillside. It was the difference between a hunch and an *informed* hunch.

Hoyt was picking up empties and chip bags in his empty parking lot. Maytubby didn't have to show him a picture of Love, and Hoyt already had phone numbers for law enforcement agencies from the Stonewall Police to Interpol. In the forty-some years he had owned the bar, he claimed to have called all of them at least once. "I ain't seen him, Bill. I eighty-sixed him a week ago. Again. Give you a ring if he turns up, which I hope he doesn't."

"'Preciate it, Hoyt."

Old 3 didn't have a sign marking the boundary between the Chickasaw and Choctaw nations, but the Coal County sign stood in for one. The Choctaw tribal police knew that Maytubby would be nosing around their bailiwick. And if it meant someone besides them would be dealing with Love, he was welcome to it.

After the old road disappeared into US 75, Maytubby looked for Jake Renaldo's cruiser in its usual concealments. He spied it in a stand of elms near Haworth Road, just outside the Coalgate city limits.

"I was hoping to find Katz here," Maytubby said.

"Even though you're in Coal County?"

"Yeah."

"Phoo-*oo!*"

"Close. But I know Katz. He's a friend of mine. And believe me, Jake, you're no Katz."

"Tidings of great joy."

"Wiley Bates still live across from the South liquor store?"

Renaldo looked south, frowned, and looked back at Maytubby.

"Bates?"

"Used to hang with Love. Roustabout."

"Can you believe Love didn't head off into the Jackfork?"

"Still might have. Only an hour away. Wiley Bates. Redhead, widow's peak, pointy nose, looks like a fox only dumber."

"Ferret, more like. I know the guy. Looks like a ferret, only meaner."

"Ferrets aren't red."

"Well, Wiley Bates doesn't have a long bushy tail, either."

"You don't know that."

"No, I don't."

Cicadas droned in the elms above the dusty cruisers.

"Does he still live across from the South Broadway liquor store?"

"I don't know that, either. Why don't you look him up on your Lighthorsemobile computer?"

"I was giving you the chance to look good."

"Thanks."

"Katz would've known where Bates lives. And he would've known he looks like a fox."

"Katz doesn't know where the president of the United States

lives. And he would have said this dude looks like a boar hog."

"Well, then, do you know where the well sites are clustered in Coal County?"

"The whole county is one big cluster. It's got a big red sweet-spot circle around it on the Woodford Shale map. 'Nother five years, that"—he looked at the ground around them—"will look like a prairie dog town. Quite a few out southwest of Lehigh, though. And talk to Lorenza Mercante. She just bought that South liquor store. Or …" Renaldo shrugged. "You can sit here till Viezer comes on at five."

Maytubby made his way south through Coalgate, whose Main Street, some decades before statehood, had been a strip mine. He passed Ole Coaly Café, the Brandin' Iron, and a good many empty storefronts.

The little clapboard cottage Maytubby recalled Bates living in looked lived in. A mint-new Bass Tracker with a fat Mercury outboard, hitch cocked up on a cinder block, gleamed in the driveway. No other vehicle. No mail in the box, no answer to Maytubby's knock. He could see the liquor store from the porch. He could also see a liquor bottle from the porch: Heaven Hill plastic magnum with a .22 hole in the neck. A "you might be a redneck if …" joke.

Lorenza Mercante beamed at Maytubby when he walked in. Her big, dark eyes widened as if they had just lit on a brother home from the war. She ran her fingers through her long black hair on their way up above her head, where they clenched into fists as she yawned. She slid off her stool—a robust woman with big, saucy lips. "Well, good morning!" she said, motioning him forward with her fingertips. "You want to know who lives in that house? 'Cause I know you don't want liquor."

"Wiley Bates?"

"Hmm." She smiled and tilted her head. It was clear she hadn't run a liquor store very long.

"He still a roustabout?"

"Yeah. He done anything wrong?"

"Not that I know of. I just wanted to ask him a few questions."

"What's a Lighthorseman doing in the Choctaw nation?"

Maytubby unfolded the mug shot. "I'm looking for this guy, Austin Love. He's a member of the Chickasaw Nation."

She inhaled sharply. "*Maledetto!*" She waved the photo away, turned toward the rear window, and began biting her nails.

"You know this man?" Maytubby folded the photo.

"Five, six years ago, I was in a club in Shawnee. Out on the Kickapoo Spur. Got crocked, went outside to be sick. Walked into some powwow—oh, sorry."

"Clandestine assembly." Maytubby smiled.

"Yeah." She squinted and smiled. "I think it was drugs. This joker"—she pointed to Maytubby's pocket—"Wolf-eyes kicked my legs out from under me. I sat right down on that muddy chat. He called me an effing you-know-what. Then he pulled me up by my hair. My *hair*! Kneed me in the ass and told me to leave. Said if I tried to go back inside he'd wear me out."

"Probably a good thing you got the beast up front. He is said to possess some charms."

Mercante wrinkled her nose and lowered her face. "*Ugh.*"

Maytubby waited.

"I guess he had kind of a striking face. Hard, though. Like painted tin. And he was the alpha dog. Wiley mixed up with this thug?"

"They ran together some years back. Not *sneakers* ran."

"Wiley is so totally a roustabout—the cowboy hard hat, the muddy pickup, the grass-stained pants and Farmer John tan—and yet he's the shape of water. Like, he comes in to buy his, uh …"

"Heaven Hill."

She slumped her shoulders and looked at him with mock dismay.

"He shot one in his yard." Maytubby tossed his head toward the front window. "Probably from inside his house."

She laughed. "His Heaven Hill. And even though he's right there in front of me, it seems like he's behind something." She passed one hand in front of the other. "After he's paid and left, he doesn't seem to of been here."

"Evanescent."

"Mister, you can put words in my mouth all day."

"You by any chance know where Wiley's working?"

Lorenza Mercante shook her fine head and shrugged. "Sorry."

"Which direction he came home from yesterday?"

She stared out the front window at Bates' house and tapped an incisor with her thumbnail.

"He comes from both directions, north and south."

"He's a roustabout. That's why I was asking about yesterday by itself."

She moved her hands as if they were puppets reliving last evening. "Judge Scarrett came in for his Springbank, four thirty-five. Court adjourned. *Hm-hm-hm* came in for her Stoli at four fifty-eight. Approximately. Jake pulled some guy over into my lot about five thirty. Wasn't one of Wiley's liquor days … South. He came from the south. If he had come in, I wouldn't have remembered that."

"You knew he wouldn't stop to make a purchase, but when you saw his truck you hoped he would, and you were disappointed."

"Yeah. Even a little pissed. Huh."

"Nice boat he's got over there."

"Shame that nasty algae closed all the lakes. I don't think he's even had it out."

"Wiley ever spring for premium bourbon?"

"You know, about the time he got that boat, three months ago, he bought Buffalo Trace. Three times. Went back to Heaven Hill. Drinkers mostly dance with the girl they brung." She said "brung" country.

A Beaver Express semi downshifted on Broadway. "What's he driving these days?"

"Red pickup. Few years old. Chevy, I think."

"Thank you very much." Maytubby tapped his brow with two fingers.

"Lorenza. Lorenza Mercante. Stop in again sometime. If you

catch Wolf-eyes, kick him in the ass for me. He falls down, help him up by his hair."

"Yes ma'am."

He was in what remained of Lehigh in ten minutes. A century had passed since this coal boomtown was an Anglo cultural hub in Indian Territory, with an opera house and a population of thousands, mostly Italian miners shipped across the Atlantic by the railroads that owned the mines. A pretty big French contingent, too. And Russians, Poles, Lithuanians, and Magyars. Choctaws owned the mineral rights, but KATY and its brethren owned the mines—and the miners, until they struck. Then the railroads brought in the freed slaves of Chickasaws and Choctaws, and freedmen from Alabama, to feed the maw.

All that remained of King Coal's sway was a single red-brick Romanesque bank building, stranded on Railway Street without a rail in sight. Maytubby admired its solemn perseverance.

West of town, he followed the section-road grid at random. Renaldo had been right: everywhere wells and tanks, and maintenance roads leading to them. On the perimeters, taut new field fence on studded T-posts. Maytubby slowed at each fresh road cut and culvert. If trees hid a well, he peered down the maintenance road or drove up it to see if Bates was cleaning the site.

The first three roustabouts Maytubby found at work drove red Chevy pickups. The fourth did, too. Maytubby could see only his back as he swung a gas Weed Eater along the perimeter fence. A tuft of red hair sprouted from beneath his tan hard hat, which was shaped like a Stetson and bore a Confederate battle flag sticker on the back of the crown. Maytubby found it amusing that Anglos deployed the Stars and Bars in Oklahoma, where almost none of them could truthfully play the heritage card.

He didn't want to startle Bates, so he leaned on the cruiser and let him work his way around the fence. Bates released the whacker throttle and stood staring through his tinted glasses at Maytubby, who gave him a friendly wave. He killed the little engine and leaned the whacker against the fence. In a second, he had disappeared behind a stand of young burr oaks.

Maytubby watched the edge of the thicket, where he thought Bates would emerge coming his way. Too much time passed. He watched for movement in the thicket.

"Help you?"

Maytubby spun to his left and faced Wiley Bates. Hard hat in hand, dusty green bandanna knotted around his neck. His pale hazel eyes just failed to make contact, focusing on nothing. The pointy nose was disturbingly musteline—Renaldo had called it: ferret.

"Hey, Wiley. You seen Austin in the last few days?"

"Nossir."

"Any idea where he's staying these days?"

"No sir." Bates was inching backward almost imperceptibly.

"When's the last time you saw him in Hoyt's?"

"Austin's eighty-sixed from Hoyt's."

"How do you know that?"

Bates stared blankly. He seemed to be receding.

"Hoyt said Austin was in his place this week," Maytubby lied.

Bates' eyes clicked down, but his sight was trained inward.

"If Hoyt was who told you Austin was eighty-sixed, he was lying to you or to me. And Hoyt doesn't need to lie to either one of us— especially to me." Maytubby entered his own lie in a fresh ledger so he could keep track of it. "If Austin told you, *you're* lying to me."

"I just heard it. Around."

"Around" was the name of that brushy plain where gossips and snitches and troublesome friends wandered in the shadows, their indistinct voices fading in the air. "'Around' stopped working in grade school, Wiley."

Maytubby glanced at the back of Bates' pickup and memorized the plate. When he looked back, the roustabout had retreated a couple of steps, though his body was still.

"Who told you?"

"I heard it when I was shootin' pool."

Maytubby strained to hear him. "Where?"

"Jeff's, over in Wapanucka."

"Jeff got rid of that coin-op table before Austin went to Mac."

"I don't know, then," Bates muttered. Plumes of Indian grass swayed across his face. Somehow, he sank beneath the stems, though it shouldn't be possible.

Maytubby flinched when the Weed Eater's two-stroke shrieked to life. A plume of blue smoke wreathed the cowboy hard hat and veiled Bates' face. Maytubby felt the haintishness of the moment, but he didn't waste the material smokescreen. He glanced into the roustabout's cab, then replayed the image as he aimed the cruiser west.

CHAPTER 9

Drifts of Sonic and Braum's wrappers and cups covered the pickup's bench seat and floorboard. Flies fastened here and there on the fresher garbage—not bad for accidental camo, but not foolproof. Maytubby had glimpsed the edge of a topo map under a Tater Tots bag, a hardwood revolver grip, the spines of several Sudafed packets. But there in plain sight, a chartreuse dream catcher lay atop the mostly white heap like an abandoned pixie snowshoe.

The dream catcher on the Cobalt had been violet. Then Maytubby recalled that he tended to misremember colors he had actually seen, as their complementary colors. He could think of no reason why Wiley Bates would have a dream catcher—much less one not hanging from his rearview mirror. He was a white male with no children and no visible girlfriend. Hell, there wasn't even a place for a woman to *sit* in his truck cab.

All he learned from the little patch of topo was that the contour lines were crowded and green. Rough forested country—not like what he was seeing out his window.

As for the packs of suzie, Love—or some other meth cook— might pay Bates and twenty others to smurf for him. The gun didn't necessarily mean anything. Everybody carried these days.

Insecure people, scared people, and the people who scared them. Wiley was likely all three.

Beyond Wapanucka, Maytubby found Hannah Bond under her favorite sycamore on the Blue. He pulled alongside her cruiser. "Brains and hash browns," he said.

"Even *I* don't eat brains."

"You heard of Raleigh Creech, over by Sulphur?"

"Gross," Bond said, turning her face away.

"So you've had the pleasure. He used to live with Austin Love's little sister. Still just might."

"Lucky girl."

"One of the state narcs told me they thought she was Austin's mule."

"If you have to go through Raleigh Creech to talk to her, you better eat first."

Maytubby held up a produce bag containing an avocado and a banana.

"*Eat*, I said. Not …" She wagged a finger at the bag.

"I showed you mine."

"I still ain't sayin'."

"Heart of ice." Maytubby saluted her as he pulled onto the highway and bit into the banana stem. He had it almost half peeled when a new white Lexus ES passed him going east. It wasn't speeding. He phoned Bond, described the car, and asked her if she had glasses and could give him the plate without pursuit.

She didn't and couldn't, except for an "X" somewhere in the middle. And it was not a specialty plate. "What do you want with the Lexus?"

"It keeps showing up. Jill said she saw it somewhere."

"Yesterday he ignored my pursuit. I didn't hit the lights. He wasn't going fast, so I fell back and followed him to Boggy Depot. He's got a country thing going on with a preacher from Tushka I had stopped before."

"Huh. Meeting a guy who rides around out here in a white

Lexus is not exactly keeping it on the down-low. You get a plate on the Lexus?"

"No. Too far away. The preacher gave me a tract."

"Are you the same Hannah you were yesterday?"

"It said, 'Satan is Waitin'.'"

"The truth shall set you free," Maytubby replied just before Bond's siren let loose.

"One-oh-eight. Lord."

*　*　*

Maytubby wound southward through the Arbuckle foothills. A very recent wildfire had incinerated a cluster of mobile homes. Scorched trampolines littered the yards like burnt spiders.

He was vaguely disappointed to see that Creech's place had been spared. The same rusted yellow Datsun 720 pickup Creech had driven years before was in the yard, within reasonable distance of the driveway. Its front half rested atop a flattened hog-wire fence, and it lacked a tailgate. The bed was smeared with what was likely the dried blood of a jacklit deer. A balled-up tarp was roped to a makeshift cleat on a wheel well. Creech was a convicted poacher and wildlife scofflaw, and his pickup was a rolling slaughterhouse.

There was no sign of the '64 Falcon Patty Love drove back then. Hounds bayed from a run of kennels on the back of the property. A log chain was bolted to an iron post in the backyard, but no pit bull.

Before Maytubby could knock on the door, Raleigh Creech appeared from behind a ramshackle outbuilding, zipping his fly. His jeans and T-shirt were stiff with filth. As he wove toward Maytubby, his face worked madly in a grotesque interplay of amusement and outrage. His thinning sandy hair stuck up like quills, and his blue-black irises looked like bullet holes. As he came nearer, Maytubby saw that Creech, not yet forty, had lost the few teeth he still had at thirty. His lips were outlined in tobacco juice.

Halting an instant before Maytubby would have to warn him, Creech held up a stiff palm. "How!"

"It's wasn't really that hard. I remembered where you live."

Creech dropped his hand and glowered. Maytubby saw that he was confused, and waited for him to speak. "Bad enough ten kinds of *white* law's always stickin' their nose in." Creech pointed over his shoulder as if some of those law were behind him. "Now here comes the redskins." He pointed at Maytubby's face, then at himself. "What I deserve, shackin' with a squaw. She's the reason you're here, right, chief? 'Cause last time I looked, I ain't no Injun."

Creech's putrid breath easily spanned the seven feet between them. Fighting the urge to back away, Maytubby held his eye. "Does Patricia Love still live here?"

Creech opened his eyes and mouth wide and shook his head. "It boggles the mind! They can find me in the futherest dark canyon of the Ouachita Mountains, but they can't find—what'd you call her?—Pa*tri*cia Love." He brayed, his purple gums shining with tobacco juice.

"Do you know where she is?"

"Roastin' in hell, I hope." Creech grinned and mimed turning a barbecue spit.

"Did she pass away?"

"Shit, I hope so, chief. I can tell you she passed away from *here*." Creech swept his arms and booted a phantom ass. The baleful glare returned. "'At whoredog was spreadin' for them spawled Dallas boys up at Lake Murray. Said she was prettyin' up ther yards. But I seen her through my rifle scope, sailin' around on ther poontang boats."

Maytubby waited.

Creech cocked his head and pointed to the log chain in his yard. "Stole my dog."

They looked at the chain.

"You seen her brother, Austin, or you know where he's living?"

He spat loudly. The tobacco juice balled up on the sand. "Dope peddler. *Indian* dope peddler. You can't get no lower'n that."

"I don't see how."

"I'll tell you where he's at. Serve her right. She sticks by her brother, even if he is trash."

Maytubby waited. A long time. Creech enjoyed having him on the hook.

"The Kiamichi makes a bend just above Antlers. Soon's you get through town on Three, leave it and go straight east on Ethel Road three miles. There's a rusted old Prince Albert sign on a post, right side of the road. Make a left and toard the river about a mile and a half. On your right you'll see a elk skull with lips painted on it, nailed up about ten feet in a burr oak. Take that right. He's back up in there."

"Thank you for your time, Mr. Creech."

He said nothing, just glowered some more.

As Maytubby drove away, Raleigh Creech stood in his rearview mirror, flipping him off with both barrels.

Maytubby frowned at the bone-dry travertine streambeds. The bank thermometer in Sulphur flashed 111. The Prince Albert sign had "fool's errand" written all over it. The joke was so old, even someone as stupid as Raleigh Creech used it. And what felon would draw attention to his house by hanging up a painted skull? A normal person wanting to deceive him would have kept a poker face and not acted like a jackanapes. But several counties lay between normal and Raleigh Creech.

The Pushmataha sheriff's deputy who took Maytubby's call from the dispatcher at the Antlers courthouse told him yes, there was indeed an old tobacco sign out that way, shot as full of holes as a cheese grater, but on State 3, not Ethel Road. The deputy's voice faded while he asked around the office about the skull. "Got two other deputies here besides me. We've seen other kinds of skulls nailed up, but not that one. You still lookin' for Love? Wait ... don't say it. That deputy Katz's been singin' that damn song since you guys lost that cranker over by Ada."

"Yes, I am."

"If he's over here, he's layin' low."

"Thanks, man."

Antlers was ninety miles east—a pretty big investment. It all hinged on Prince Albert. Maytubby shook his head at that mental sentence. Did Creech just remember that sign from some poaching expedition? Or was he telling the truth and just forgot what road it was on?

On his way east, he found Bond parked in the shade just outside Wapanucka. "Calf fries and scrambled."

"Even *I* don't eat calf fries."

"Make you tall and strong."

"You calling me a liar?"

"Hannah, nobody's going to have enough road to reach the speed limit, much less break it."

"Psychological warfare."

"I talked to Raleigh Creech."

"He spit on your boots?"

"No, but he smelled like last week's roadkill. Said he kicked Love's sister out for cheating on him."

Bond's piercing laugh was startling and infectious.

"He spied on her with his rifle scope," Maytubby said through giggles. She laughed harder. "Said he saw her riding in a 'poontang boat.'"

Bond was pink now and pounding the cruiser's headliner. When she caught her breath, she said, "'Course he did," and wiped her eyes. Her giggles returned. "Probably a Crappie Pro."

"Camo," he blurted as he fell into a wheezing laugh.

Passing motorists stared at them. They took a while to catch their breath.

"Creech told me Love is holed up on the Kiamichi, by Antlers. Said he was telling me to get back at Patty Love. I asked some cops there about the landmarks in his directions. Some are where

Creech puts them. Nobody's seen Love, except maybe the woman in Stratford who said she saw him in Ardmore."

"You believe that subhuman?"

"His stalking tale was so good, I feel like I owe him."

"So you *don't* believe him?"

"Not really." Glancing at Bond's radar readout, which was flashing really pitiful numbers in the thirties, Maytubby was reminded of the white Cobalt. "Hey, what did that preacher you stopped look like?"

"Stick-up red hair, kind of thin. Top shirt button buttoned. Oh, something about one of his eyes." She looked at Maytubby's face. "Left eye. It kind of …" With her left thumb and index finger she drew an imaginary extension of her eye toward her temple.

"I think I've seen this fellow before. Show me his DPS photo." She clicked at her computer until a photo popped up. "That's the guy. He was driving an old gray pickup like the one the Stratford woman said Love was driving in Ardmore. Specifically, the redhead was driving a gray-primered '66 Ford."

"Plate?"

"Intentionally ignored it because I thought the woman was lying."

"Mm."

"I know. Was there a dream catcher hanging from the rearview mirror?"

"No."

"Plate?"

She scrolled down her records and gave it to him. He memorized it. "Name and address for the license?"

He tried not to lead the witness. "Anything physically unusual about the plate?"

She looked down and to her right. "Didn't look fake. Paint was even. Lot of dust."

"Had the dust settled evenly on it?"

"Oh, man." Bond sighed and put her hand over her mouth. A car passed doing eighteen miles an hour. "There were darker patches—square, matter of fact."

"Like what duct tape for a lost license plate would make."

She nodded.

"Your preacher might have been driving the white Cobalt we think picked up Love when we were chasing him in the Kullihoma grounds."

Bond tapped at her computer, handed Maytubby a slip of paper with the driver's name, David Woodley, and his address on South Jefferson in Tushka. When he read the street name, the driver's name set off a distant tintinnabulation, which in turn reminded him to ask if Bond remembered the dealer logo."

"All I remember is, I couldn't make sense of the spelling. Some weird name."

"F-U-S-I-L-I-E-R?"

She shrugged.

"You run the VIN?"

"No. Here." She tapped on her keyboard. "This car was purchased by Woodley in Jennings, Louisiana."

"From Bubba Fusilier."

"Is Woodley a Cajun name?"

"I doubt it. David Woodley was an LSU quarterback who went pro. Played for Miami and Pittsburgh in the eighties. Died in the early aughts."

"Sounds fishy, huh?"

"Yep. But why pick a famous name as your alias?"

"He looks young enough, he might have heard the name but not connected it to the player."

"True. Or maybe a little inside joke he could risk because he thought Woodley was such a dinosaur, nobody would remember him."

"Anything on him?"

She tapped some more. "No."

"Did Waitin' Satan have a church address stamped on his back page?"

"I didn't read that far." She pulled open the ashtray and plucked out the paper ball, gave it to Maytubby. He pulled on some latex gloves, slowly unpacked the ball, and spread the pages flat against his palm. At the bottom of the back page, in a blank space reserved for the church's name and address, a red-inked rubber stamp had skidded a little when it hit the page: *Sun Ray Gospel Fellowship.* "Hannah, could you Google this Oklahoma City address?"

Sweat stung his eyes as he leaned in to look at her computer screen. "The Sun Ray Fellowship isn't two blocks from the Western Sky Motel. You remember, that's one of the places Tate called on her disposable cell." Bond turned up the cruiser AC. She got the street view, and they peered at a tattered building that had, in some former life, been a fast-food restaurant. Its steel awnings, peeling several coats and colors of paint, winged away from their boxy fuselage. In yellow tempera paint, a stylized sunrise radiated beams across the broad canted plate glass of the tiny dining room. The name of the church was spelled out in red blocked capitals between the sun rays. They Googled for a website and found none, only some fragmentary references to the church.

"Are there circuit preachers anymore?" Hannah said.

"Some little churches need them. Some of my family go to churches with circuit preachers."

"Might explain how Woodley met White Lexus."

"What is this, *Pride and Prejudice*? While you're at Google Maps ..." He pointed to the radar readout. "Six miles an hour. Really? Could we have a street view of Woodley's address in Tushka?"

The Google camera car had visited Tushka when a nasty thunderstorm loomed in the southwest. As the cursor jerked down Jefferson Street, the town's main drag, they could see lightning bolts in some frames. "Cool," Maytubby said.

Bond held a flat palm toward the screen. "You think somebody lives in that?"

The image was three years old, so Maytubby didn't bother looking at the driveway or the mailbox. He did see that three years ago, the Atoka County Health Department had posted an orange condemnation notice on the house at that address.

He shook his head. "Not much help. At least Tushka's on the road to Antlers. I'll put Woodley's vehicle and plate out there."

Bond's radar buzzed, blinking 52. Maytubby backed away from her cruiser as her strobes came on.

"See?" She leaned toward him, pointing a thumb at the speeder. "I mess with their minds."

CHAPTER 10

Maytubby never passed up a chance to take Chicken Fight Road, which was to Oklahoma as Music Street was to New Orleans. It made a little shortcut to US 69, the truck-hammered Tulsa-to-Dallas conduit that, for a quarter mile, became the main drag of Tushka, a town best known locally as the site of the Choctaw stomp grounds. His turn indicator clicked monotonously as dozens of rumbling semis passed going the other way, blocking a left turn into the porte cochère chez Woodley. His between-trucks glimpses of the place showed that the condemnation notice had not moved and that the weeds growing in the driveway ruts were waist high.

On the porch, he squinted under his hand. No furniture inside—nothing but blistered linoleum, an empty shoe box with no lid, and a scattering of rat turds. Nothing in the backyard but a curious neighbor at the shared cyclone fence. Maytubby waved at him and asked if he knew who owned the house and if anyone had lived here recently.

The thin man of seventy or so, shirtless, in clean chinos held up by green galluses, pointed to the house. "That house," he said regally, "airn' inhabited. Ner has it been since the owner was diseased. Her name was Opal Noll. She was the dead end of her race."

Maytubby thanked the man and kicked the cruiser over some section roads, rejoining Oklahoma 3 at Darwin and crawling through downtown Antlers, past the Phoenix Theatre and Pirate Bail Bonds. He stopped for the only traffic light in Pushmataha County. Ethel Road tunneled into the Kiamichi's riparian thicket and occasionally emerged into a bright clearing.

A Rustin Concrete plant coated the tree leaves with gray dust for a half mile. Maytubby had read that when H. C. Rustin founded the business in the 1950s, he gave all the credit to Jesus Christ, who had sent him dreams with every detail of the business he was chosen to build—right down to the floor plan.

When he reached the dead end of Ethel Road without finding Prince Albert in or on a can, Maytubby looked for him on 3. On his third pass over a three-mile stretch, he saw a sliver of bullet-riddled rust leaning against a fence post: a silhouette of the prince, no taller than a ten-year-old. Maytubby had been looking for a billboard. From it, only one road led toward the river: the same one he had driven down from Ethel. Back up it he went, crossing Ethel and keeping his eye peeled for elk antlers.

The road shrank to a pair of ruts and juked as it neared the river. When the yellow DEAD END sign appeared around a bend, he resolved to go home. It was getting dusky. He backed to do a bootleg turn. Two points into the three-point turn, there was the skull, up in a burr oak, lips painted on it, just as Creech had said. It crossed Maytubby's mind that such a thing might be the country relative of tennis shoes on a telephone wire. It would mean lots of weird encounters at deer camps. The shale-crunching turn didn't do much for the cause of stealth, but a cop driving a shiny black Charger with LIGHTHORSE stenciled on the fender didn't have much to lose. Still, out of habit, he backed the cruiser around the bend from the drive and into some underbrush.

The dirt drive turned upward, away from the river, and disappeared into some pines. Sometime long ago when there was rain, the drive had spilled sand over the county road's chat. Many cars had passed the drive since anyone drove in or out of it.

Maytubby told his dispatcher what he was doing. She could see exactly where he was—could call in the coordinates to vaporize the place or his car.

He opened his car door, and the heat rolled over him. It would still be over a hundred at nine. He left his campaign hat on the seat and tied the blue bandanna around his crown. He could work better without the head oven, and he liked the flair of rebellion. Walking along the drive, he saw, between recent tread marks, little patches imprinted by the thick Ground Hawg lugs. Tread design matched the prints in Majesty Tate's drive. So Love had likely been here sometime before Nub Jump's mules dragged his pickup out of Kullihoma. Likely after, too, in one of the other vehicles.

Maytubby pulled the little tape measure and digital camera out of his shirt pocket, laid the tape over the tread marks, and photographed them. One of the treads might have been the low-end Cobalt, which wore a 195mm—about eight inches. He walked into the woods and paralleled the drive, pausing now and then to listen. Nothing but birdsong and distant river sounds. The shadows deepened but didn't cut the heat at all.

It was a long driveway. After topping the little river bluff, it fell again toward the river before it reached a cottage someone had started decades ago and never finished. Tar paper peeled off the stained plywood walls, and warped window frames bugged out on every side. The roof was covered with Visqueen anchored by stones. A zany stovepipe canted dangerously over the plastic sheeting. The house had no electric service. There were no meth RVs or any other vehicles. The only outbuilding was an outhouse, distinguished by a paneled door painted orange. Everybody in the house would have to pass through it, so Maytubby studied the footprints. Herman Survivors had certainly marched in this parade.

The windows were not blacked out, as Maytubby had expected, but hung with rotten bedsheets and canvas tarpaulin. Missing panes had been replaced by chunks cut from Styrofoam ice chests and taped in place. He knocked on the front door and announced himself. Not even a creak. He looked into every room and saw no camp stoves or ammonia bottles or tubing in any of them. No spoons or syringes. People had been living here.

Torn blankets, scored by slivers of evening sunlight, lay over the two foul mattresses in both rooms, and cast-off men's clothes littered the floor. A Franklin woodstove stood in the center of the house, with skillets on both lids. In the kitchen sink, which was served by a hand pump built into the counter, crusted pans and open food cans were piled as high as they could go. Fast-food litter covered the dining table and much of the floor. Possibly a hundred empty liquor bottles lay on the floor. A kerosene lamp with a smutched globe stood on an upended fruit crate. Some empty boxes of Marlboro reds gaped on top of the trash. Love's brand, but that didn't mean much. At least Maytubby wouldn't have to dig through the trash.

For all its Pap Finn squalor, the place was disappointingly light on evidence of criminal enterprise—no guns, no booty, no needles, no sticks of dynamite. But the men who slept here did not have regular jobs. It wasn't clear how often they slept here. The crust on the pots and cans was hard and cracked. Mice scurried over the Sonic and Burger Barn wrappers.

Out on the road, chat popped. Maytubby sprinted into the brush and toward the sound, hoping to get a glimpse of the vehicle. Brambles snared his legs twice, sent him sprawling on hot earth. And the house was a long way from the road. Nearing the last rise before the hill fell to the road, he heard the vehicle—by its sound, a small car—accelerate quickly and spin on the gravel. Chat buckshot clattered against the DEAD END sign. The driver had seen the cruiser.

Maytubby broke through a stand of redbud saplings and out into the road. The fleeing car was veiled by dust. All he could say for certain was that it was a light-colored compact. It had slewed through the dirt at the end of the driveway, erasing its own tread marks.

When the cruiser was jolting over the shale at forty, he snatched off his bandanna and wiped his face and neck with it. At Edna Road, which was paved, he looked all three directions, saw no dust plume on the unpaved road straight ahead of him, and decided on Edna Road west, which led toward HQ in Ada. As he passed fifty, he noticed, out of the corner of his eye, a dusting of bright litter on the right. He stopped quickly, fired the strobes, and backed down the grass shoulder until the cruiser was on top of the mess. He opened his door and snatched up a folded sheet of slick paper inked red and white. Satan was in the red. And he was waitin'. Maytubby had just paid a visit to the Reverend Woodley's parsonage.

After rebroadcasting the Cobalt's possible connection to Love, its plate number, and a description of Woodley, Maytubby hit Oklahoma 3 for the eighty-mile trip. He charged his cell from the cruiser's lighter. After filling up at a new prefab truck stop in Atoka, he called Les Fox, who told him that neither medical examiner nor Feds had said boo all day. Then he called Jill Milton, told her where he was, and asked if ten thirty would be too late for a visit.

"For a visit, yes."

"How about a quote *vis*it?"

"It would not be too late for that. Oh, hey!"

"Yes?"

"I remembered where I saw that white Lexus—or its twin. Solomon Stoddard was driving it in Paoli."

"Something to chew on."

"As you traverse the darkling plain."

"As I drive through Tupelo."

A bank thermometer blinked an orange 101 when Maytubby slowed into Coalgate. Evening chill. He glanced at Wiley Bates' house. It was dark, even the porch. Bates' pickup was gone. His boat was gone. It was not the weekend.

Maytubby braked, made a U-turn on South Broadway, and pulled up to Lorenza Mercante's liquor store. It was ten o'clock—

closing time for all liquor stores in the state—and she was dropping a two-by-four into its cradles, barring the door. Seeing Maytubby get out of his cruiser, she brought the board back up so he could come inside.

"I saw you go past and then turn around right quick," she said. "I know what you want." She tossed her head toward Bates' house. "Wish it was something else. He emptied his house into his pickup about an hour ago, hitched up the new boat." She smiled at him.

"Wha ...?"

"Just messin' with you. North, this time."

"Thanks a lot, Ms. Mercante."

"Lorenza. What's going on?"

He stared at his and Mercante's reflections in the plate glass. Headlights on the highway flashed across Bates' windows. "I wish I knew."

"Wolf Eyes still on the loose?"

"Unless he fell down a well."

"You're still going to kick his ass for me, right?"

"Yes, ma'am."

She smiled.

CHAPTER 11

After a day of driving through the poorest counties in Oklahoma, Maytubby felt a jolt of disorientation when his headlights swept the Tudor, Georgian, and Spanish colonial mansions that studded the crown of King's Road. The Fittstown boom of 1934 had built most of them, their oil-patch upstart owners now long dead. Long dead the chauffeur who first occupied the garage apartment where Jill Milton now lived. Gone to rust the yellow Bentley or Duesenberg or whatever he once steered.

Through Jill's front door, he could hear the identifier for KGOU, the Norman NPR station that Chickasaw Enterprises helped string to Ada. When he knocked, the radio volume went down, and Jill greeted him with a blinding smile. She was wearing a sunset jersey shift and no shoes. Her apartment smelled like oranges. A five-string banjo sat upright on her couch.

She squeezed his abs. "Avocado and, what, raisins? Apple?"

"Banana."

"Maybe we should switch jobs."

"It's the twenty-first century," he said. "I am not wearing panty hose."

"See?"

"Hannah Bond wouldn't tell me what she had for breakfast this morning at the Downtown Diner in Tish. Said it's because you're a dietitian. I think you pose a serious risk to my social well-being."

"That'll be the day. I bet it was brains."

"She was pretty definite on that one—doesn't eat brains."

Jill Milton took a bowl of bulgur, mint, and onion salad out of her refrigerator and handed it to Maytubby. "Was she still at the diner when she said that?"

"Yeah."

"Okay, we'll give her that one."

"Such a simple thing, I ..."

"Bull. She knows the only reason you ask is that you're envious, and she pretends to be embarrassed to spare you from facing your own dietary smugness."

He took a spoon from the counter and twiddled it, watching her. "She said the same thing about calf fries, but she was in Wapanucka."

"You asked her a*gain?*"

"We're not giving her that one," Maytubby said, going to work on the bulgur.

"Hear anything from the medical examiner or the FBI?"

He shook his head. "Dis is ..."

"Isn't it? I have to make it in the demonstration kitchen. They'll laugh at me and tell me it looks like dirt. Austin Love still at large?" She peeled an orange and stacked the parings on her finger-pick box.

Maytubby reached in his uniform pocket with his free hand and held the unserved tribal court warrant over his head.

"Woman in Stratford used to know him, claimed she saw him driving an old gray pickup in Ardmore."

"That and a nickel get you a streetcar ride."

"I thought so, too. But first thing out of Stratford, I see a gray-primered old Ford pickup driven by this odd-looking fellow with Johnny Rotten hair and one eye casing his sideburn. Hannah stopped the same guy later in the day, driving a Cobalt like the one Jake and I think picked up Love at Kullihoma. Said he was a preacher in Tushka, name on the license Woodley. He gave her a tract titled 'Satan is Waitin'.' Church name stamped on the back is a tiny mission in the city. Wait …" He raised his left palm and downed a few more mouthfuls of bulgur. "A new white Lexus like—or *the* one—Stoddard was driving passed her, going a little fast. She followed at a distance, said the driver was mad about something. Eventually, the white Lexus and Woodley rendezvoused at Boggy Depot. Hannah thought they were on the down-low, and let 'em be. I checked the good reverend's address in Tushka—empty for years."

The apartment's tiny window unit shuddered off. They watched it until it revived—twenty seconds. Then they relaxed.

Maytubby told her about the Love sighting outside Hoyt's in Stonewall, Wiley Bates' new boat, and his hasty move. Lorenza Mercante he left out, not because Jill Milton was a jealous person—she wasn't—but because he made a living watching faces and he knew, if he tried to keep even a shopkeeper he didn't know out of his face, he would fail because she was a fetching woman. He related Hannah's interview with Love's uncle, Raleigh Creech's surprising hot tip, and the waitin'-Satan pamphlets blown out of a car fleeing his pursuit near Antlers.

"You put in 'hot tip' and 'fleeing pursuit' for me, huh?"

"I never pander."

"What, never?"

"No. Never."

"Never?"

"Well, hardly ever."

"So, you've put Love in Mill Creek, Stonewall, maybe in Antlers, but now …"

Maytubby turned his palms up. "Everybody's looking for him—and now for the Cobalt. I'm just looking a little harder."

"Bates ran with him back in the day; uncle was uncle; Creech lived with his sister. What do you make of the others?

Maytubby washed his bowl and spoon, put them on a drying rack. "I think they may be in cahoots."

"If not, they're wasting a lot of time together."

"There was no meth stuff around that place in Antlers. We got no plate on the white Lexus, though I can find that. Still, my guess is, the glue that holds them together is a dangerous controlled substance."

"You really think, if Stoddard's the owner of that Lexus, he's cranking or dealing while fighting a holy war?"

"Maybe he has a weight problem."

"Maybe Hannah was right and he was just hooking up with Woodley," Jill said. She licked orange from her fingers, picked a round bamboo tea tray up off the coffee table, and fanned herself. Then she fanned in Maytubby's direction. "You want some?"

"Yes. The State Senate district Stoddard gave up last year is really close to the Sun Ray Gospel Fellowship, whose tracts the quote Reverend Woodley was handing out. And Majesty Tate called rooms at two old motels close to both."

"This Woodley fellow, if that's his name, apparently isn't even from here. No record. Why would he help Love? Did Love teach him to cook? Hook him up with his old clientele? You think Love has something on him? They have prison friends in common?"

"All possible. But those scenarios sound too complicated for Austin Love. He just had a little drinking gang, got in fights, then later probably cooked meth and sold it around. Certainly toted a shitload of it. He was always sort of a gregarious loner."

"You mean he was alone in himself but needed company?"

"Exactly. He mostly worked independently. Probably why he and his friends were in county jails together for smashing up taverns, but he went to prison for peddling, while his friends stayed outside. Here, give me that."

She Frisbeed the tray over the table, and he slapped it straight up and plucked it from the air. He fanned her in slow motion, and she mock-glowered at him.

"You and Hannah still think Love acted alone," Jill said.

"Oh, yeah. Tate was last seen alive at a bar in Sulphur. Love entered the place alone. Everyone who saw her and Love there said the couple appeared to share a mutual affection."

"They didn't say that."

"Not precisely. They said, 'Them two couldn't keep their hands off each other.' People in Bromide saw Love's monster truck and its driver going up and down the road to Tate's house. His tire prints—now we have his truck and a match—are all over her yard. I found a bloody knife that looks like one he always wore. He stole gas from his uncle's truck the night of the murder. Has a history of battering women. He fled when pursued by officers from three different agencies."

Maytubby pulled the enlarged mug of Love out of his bulging pocket, unfolded it, and held it out.

Jill grimaced. "Plus, he looks really scary. I have new admiration for Hannah's restraint."

"She may let you down."

"I hope so."

He stowed Love's mug shot. "I take it the demonstration kitchen was spared the wrath of Stoddard and his toadies."

"Are you kidding? Ten women in a kitchen, canning fruit?"

Maytubby nodded. "Utopia."

"And wearing aprons."

"Gingham?"

"As a matter of fact."

"Panty hose?"

She shook her head. "Shhh. Don't tell." She went to the counter and brought back a Mason jar packed with peaches.

He looked at the fruit and winced. "Stratford, huh?"

She nodded.

"Drought'll take the varnish off utopia."

"Kept the camera operator busy switching angles to hide the flaws."

"Couldn't you just bring in some ringers from Save-a-Lot? I mean, not even the cattle are eating local this summer."

"You watch too many food shows."

"I don't even own a television."

"True. Maybe you watch too many food shows on your computer."

"I don't know how to watch television on my computer."

"Oh, yeah … Well, I got to put my education to work this afternoon. Nurse called from the Nation Medical Center about a predialysis renal diet."

The window unit quaked to a halt. The brief hush was filled by a sibilant chorus of sprinkler arrays in the odd-numbered lawns of King's Road houses.

"Did she call you 'Dr. Milton'?"

"He. No. 'Jill.' I know him. Besides, it's a hospital. You have to be a *real* doctor."

"Did you know I am a tribal cop?"

"You mean you're not a *real* cop? Damn. All this time, I'm thinking you're my ticket to respectability."

"I'm afraid we're a coupla' quacks."

She rose and took his hand, pulled until he rose, exactly to her height: five-ten. "We'll just have to make the best of a bad situation." They hugged hard. "You can stay?"

Maytubby nodded.

"You better."

They leaned against each other and looked out her kitchen window at the points of golden sodium light atop Chimney Hill.

"When this place was built, there was nothing but moonlight on that land," she said.

"You didn't have to come back here. How often you think about Brooklyn?"

"You didn't have to come back, either. Some days, when I'm doing the Eagle Play with the kids or working against a grant deadline, I don't." She spread her hand toward the window. "The land smells like home. Especially sycamore and cedar and alfalfa. Big sky, quiet. I do miss the cloak of invisibility. My NYU friends.

The collective energy. In small towns, personal force can mean too much. And there aren't enough different kinds of prejudice to neutralize each other."

"Or enough noodle shops."

"Or *any* noodle shops."

"Yeah, but let me ask you this: Can you go to cowboy church in Brooklyn?"

"That's why I love you, man. You always make me feel good about my life choices."

"And if you had stayed in Brooklyn, you might be shacking up with a tattooed fire-eater from Texarkana."

"I take back what I said. I really miss that dude."

"Oh, yeah? What was his name?"

She stuck out her chin. "Dude."

She pushed him into the tiny bathroom. "Take a shower."

CHAPTER 12

"Bill ... Bill." Jill Milton jostled his shoulder.

He muttered something, was quiet for a second, then sat upright in bed. "I'm awake," he said loudly as he gazed around him like a crash victim trying to put together what just happened.

"It's your cell." She pointed to the nightstand on his side, where a glowing rectangle was crawling, blaring the phone's factory ring tone. Only faint slivers of blue dawn light were bleeding through the old venetian blinds. *Drapes of lath,* for Okies, he fleetingly recalled. He stared at the cell phone for three seconds, then snatched it up. "Hannah," he said. Jill watched his glowing blue face. "Really. You call the state? Forty-eight-A at Kite Road, then west to the end. Be there in thirty minutes."

"She found Love."

Maytubby fumbled with his shirt buttons. "Yeah. He's down on the Blue. Ran from her." Maytubby had one pant leg on when his ham knotted up. He danced in pain, trying to straighten his leg.

"Don't tense your leg. Straighten it and curl your toes." Jill put her strong hands to work, kneading the cramp. Her focus frown reminded him of a toddler solving a puzzle.

He breathed deeply, leaning on the nightstand, and let her slip his service trousers on him. He put on his boots and duty belt, managed a fleeting kiss. The strange early commotion had stirred them. She trailed him out of the room, her hand on his back. At the refrigerator, she pinched his shirt and held him back while she fished out a banana and a Mason jar half full of peach juice. She held them out to him. "Go."

*　*　*

At the end of the driveway, he passed through tall cast-iron gates that were rusted open. Stopping at King's Road, he noticed the headlights of a compact car stopped fifty yards up the hill. After a few seconds, the car made a U-turn and disappeared over the hill. Maytubby turned left instead of right and followed the car. When he came over the hill, its brake lights were almost in his grille. He hit the brakes and swerved around a white Fiesta. In his rearview mirror, he could see a fat newspaper spinning end over end into a tree-lined driveway. *Dallas Morning News*. He hissed at himself and took the back way to the Ada bypass.

Had he slept at home, he could have dropped by HQ to get the four-by-four on his way down. But Jill's house was several miles closer to Austin Love. At 6:40, just before sunrise, he got off the Ada bypass at Ahloso and headed due south on US 377, strobes and siren all code red—to keep himself awake as much as to warn the ranchers and roustabouts asleep at the wheel before their country store coffee. He never drove as fast as the cops he knew. Even in his few years as a Lighthorseman, he had seen too many men, women, and children killed by speed. As the light came, he searched the road's margins for deer.

What was Hannah Bond doing before dawn that she would come across Austin Love? Her shift didn't even start till seven. And how did she spot Love in the dark? A traffic stop? Maytubby was surprised she hadn't shot him or pursued him alone into the woods along the Blue—even in the dark. She gave no quarter to men who hurt women. It was a shame so many brutes were too wasted at the time to remember who had taken them down in their own homes.

Maytubby called the LHP dispatcher and told her what he was up to. He asked her which officers in the vicinity would be on duty by 7:00 a.m. She said none. He asked her to call the OHP and see if they couldn't get an officer on Prairie Road just south of 377 and 7, on the side opposite Love's entry into the forest surrounding the Blue. He gave her the description of the Cobalt and its plate number. He didn't want a replay of Kullihoma. Bond would have gotten any available Johnston deputies into the game and might also have called OHP. Renaldo was out of Troop E in Durant and didn't do Johnston County. That was Troop F, in Ardmore. Maytubby finished off his banana and peach juice. They were sweet and healthy. But he began to imagine sitting down with Hannah Bond to biscuits and black-pepper gravy.

He crossed the Blue on State 7, the Belton Bridge, at Hannah Bond's favorite speeder blind. Taking the next paved right, 48A, he drove south two miles, then turned off the pavement and back west, toward the river, on Kite Road. Bond's cruiser was parked in an alder grove, blocking the 1966 gray-primered Ford pickup, which had eaten about three inches of persimmon bark.

It was full light and already hot. Machinery in a gravel pit to the north grumbled and raised a white plume of dust. Before Bond got to the Lighthorse cruiser, Maytubby had shed his boots and campaign hat and duty belt and tied on his bandanna. He stuck his pistol in his belt, and two pairs of PlastiCuffs, a pair of field glasses, and a pint flask of water in his pants pocket, then turned down the volume on his shoulder radio. An earpiece would muffle a hemisphere of sounds. He rose and shut the door softly.

Bond stared at him. She was still shaking her head when she fell in behind Maytubby, going the direction Love had fled. "I heard you dressed like that in a chase," she whispered. "You look plumb retarded."

As long as there was at least a little sand, the Herman Survivor boot prints were as good as trail markers.

Bond whispered, "We've got an unmarked pickup down near the end of that trail between here and the Blue. Deputy's off the trail. I can text him. OHP just south of Seven on Three Seventy-Seven."

Maytubby nodded. If Love walked straight and fast, he couldn't reach 377 in less than an hour from the time Maytubby and Bond gave chase. The Survivor prints appeared so regularly, Maytubby began to jog. Bond was no slouch on the course. She even had to check her longer stride to stay behind him. Every few minutes, he halted abruptly when he lost sign, forcing her to grab his shoulders so she didn't bowl him over.

They skirted a bald knoll. From shadows at the edge of the knob, Maytubby used the height to look at the route he took in—to make sure Love's chauffeur wasn't circling around behind his back.

They picked up Love's trail on the other side of the hill and slid down a pebbly cut to Peter Sandy Creek. The bed was dry but shaded. Love hadn't even bothered to hide his path.

On the other side of the creek, the underbrush thickened: brambles, possum berry, poison oak. Love had ceased to cut trail and had taken the cow path of least resistance, for which Maytubby was warily grateful. The last time out, Love had planned to let him drive right past him. But for now, there were the prints, big as day. A smoldering Marlboro butt. He jogged faster, slaloming around noisy deadwood.

They approached another rise, this one wooded. Near the top, Maytubby slowed and bent at the waist. He turned to see if they were high enough to catch a view of the roads they had taken in. Just barely. Bond knew what he was doing, and bent away to clear his line of vision. Nothing. At the crest of the hill, they crouched and listened. He glassed the woods in every direction. A few crows called as they careened south on their crazy wing beats. Down the other side they jogged, still on the cow path. Their uniform shirts were soaked. Maytubby wrung out his do-rag as he jogged. Bond's khaki ball cap was soaked right up to its button. When they reached the unimproved road coming south from State 7, there was no sign of the unmarked pickup in either direction, and they could see easily a half mile. The deputy might still be farther north or south. Love's prints went right across the road, and so did they.

Even drought throttled, the Blue managed a decent rumble at the Desperado Spring falls. The sound made them both wildly thirsty. Their water flasks came out, and they drank as they jogged through the last thousand yards of oaks and native elms before the river. On the bank below the falls, they knelt and splashed their faces. Maytubby and Bond saw at once that Love's tracks did not appear on the opposite bank. Each checked the bank on one side of the falls, saw nothing. Nothing looked disturbed along the lip of the falls. Maytubby pointed downstream, and Bond nodded. Each took a side and waded or walked the bank, looking for the tracks to emerge. The spring-fed river water felt good on Maytubby's feet. He doubted that Hannah, slogging in her boots, felt the same way. In winter, the river stayed cold enough for long enough that the state stocked it with trout.

Emerging from a chute with steep banks, they saw that the stream broke into three channels around two islands. Just before they tackled that problem, Hannah tossed a pebble at Maytubby, who turned and saw her pointing to Love's tracks emerging on the west. Pointing this way and that, he indicated that she should follow the tracks and he would continue down the river on his side. He held up five fingers for how many minutes they should go their separate ways. She nodded.

A great blue heron, fishing off one of the islands, dipped at the knees and sprang into the draft of its vast wings. A path followed the river here, and Maytubby made good time in his two and a half minutes. Like any kid and most adults, he broke the time rule because he hadn't finished his game. At four minutes, he found Love's footprints coming out of the river, headed back east. The time problem then solved itself. Hannah would not turn back after two and a half if she saw Love's prints turn toward the river.

Maytubby sat on a shady rock and waited two minutes. Bond strode out of a blackberry patch, holding her arms above her head. For a half second, Maytubby was alarmed; then he realized she was protecting her arms and hands against the fishhook thorns. She shook her head before nodding at her friend to lead the way. His hunches irked her.

Love's detour almost a mile south in the river meant they could not have seen him returning east. They easily followed his trail—he was in a hurry now—and they went fast, Bond's boots squishing. Maytubby whispered back to Bond to tell the OHP officer to go to the intersection of Sardis Road and 48A, and the unmarked pickup deputy to go to the intersection of 48A and State 7. She called OHP first, speaking softly into her shoulder radio between breaths.

An engine started not far ahead of them. They both looked up from the trail. The sound of gravel ricocheting off metal, then some yelling. Maytubby ran faster. A pistol shot, then a second. The sound of the pickup dopplered and faded.

"The county's Silverado," Bond said aloud, for there was no longer any need to whisper. "You go on." She waved for emphasis. As he moved farther from her, she shouted, "I'll phone OHP dispatch to get their man to Belton Bridge where this track hits Seven, tell him about the Silverado. Love can't go fast on that trail, and he can hear our radio." Maytubby raised his arm in acknowledgment and ticked up his pace. Shortly, he could see the road cut and a Johnston County deputy—a young one he didn't know—standing in the road, holding his pistol against his thigh. The air smelled faintly of sycamore and burnt powder.

Maytubby stopped well back from the road, in the trees, snapped off his bandanna, and shouted, "Lighthorse Police!" Before the second word the deputy had spun and raised his weapon. It twitched. "Come on out," the deputy said. As Maytubby walked slowly toward the verge of the clearing, watching the pistol, the deputy's radio came alive with Hannah's voice. "Eph, don't shoot Sergeant Maytubby. He's ahead of me."

With some difficulty, Eph holstered his gun. His face was red, and his shirt was wet as a dishrag. He fidgeted. Maytubby walked slowly toward him.

"Sorry, Sergeant. That skeleton freak stole the department's unmarked vehicle." His eyes grew wide as he took in Maytubby's bare feet. "D'he steal your boots, too?"

"He sure did, the sly bastard. And I aim to get 'em back."

Bond jogged into the clearing. She had her cell phone out, aiming the camera at Eph. "Your spent brass?" she said.

He stood next to them. She said, "Point north." He did, and she took a photo for his report. All three of them were off at a good jog up the track. When they reached the spot where Maytubby and Bond had crossed the track, Bond told Eph to continue up the track to the highway to make sure Love had not detoured or abandoned the pickup. Then Maytubby and Bond jogged east back down to Peter Sandy Creek.

"F?" Maytubby said.

"Ephraim," she said.

"As in 'Asher,' 'Dan,' 'Gad.'"

"Yep. Tribe … of … Israel," she panted.

"Like 'Maytubby.'"

"Mm-hm."

They slowed into the small clearing and walked to the vehicles.

"I need to disable the pickup," Maytubby said.

"Yo," Bond called to him, pulling its coil wire from her pants pocket.

He nodded, gave her a thumbs-up, pulled his emergency water jug from his cruiser trunk. "You got a tea bag?" he said as he filled Bond's flask.

They stood panting in the shade of the persimmon tree Love's truck had bitten. She drank slowly. "*Ach*. It *is* hot. But I wouldn't care if it was boiling." She cell-phoned Eph to remind him that Love could hear the radio. He was walking to meet a ride on State 7.

Maytubby filled his flask and drank deep. "Hannah, I don't

think Love's going on the road. The state'll have an APB by now. He knows he wouldn't get three miles, even if he doesn't know that truck has a GPS locator. I think he'll go back in, but not as far down as the Wildlife Area campsites—on this side of the river. We can go in from the South on Bold Springs Road.

"You figure?" They drank and listed to a mockingbird running through its repertoire. Bond was not convinced. She had found him and didn't want to lose him.

"I'm going down there. Wanna come?"

"How is Love going to get down there?"

"Turn around."

"Eph'll shoot him."

Maytubby walked quickly toward his cruiser. "Yeah."

Bond's cell buzzed, and Maytubby stopped. After she said "Bond," a hornet din spilled from the phone. She held it back from her ear and mouthed, "Let's go," to Maytubby as she jumped in her cruiser. "Easy, Eph," he heard her say before she closed her door.

As they sped south down 48A, Maytubby called Ardmore OHP dispatch on his cell and told them to move their trooper to the west of the river, the intersection of Bullard Chapel Road and Harbert Road. He explained what was going on, and reminded the dispatcher about the white Cobalt. He again supplied the plate.

Turning west on Bold Springs, Maytubby watched Bond's cruiser through the plume of dust he was kicking up. The road wound a bit, then headed due north toward a hairpin in the Blue, where it forded the river on a low-water crossing. Just shy of the river, Maytubby and Bond parked their cruisers on either side of the road for whatever scarecrow effect they might have.

Tying on his damp bandanna as he walked fast, Maytubby slid down into the dry bed of Peter Sandy Creek, with Bond right behind him. They climbed up the other bank on exposed blackjack roots and began to jog over a flat clearing. "Why didn't Eph shoot Love?" Maytubby whispered.

"He thought somebody else was coming down the track. He

was going to wave 'em down. Love came around the bend so fast, Eph had to dive out of the way. Landed on a prickly pear. He was mad as a cut snake."

"Did he turn around and follow the pickup?"

"Yeah."

"Good … I think."

They slowed a bit, stopped now and then to listen. The river, on their left, masked any sound short of a gunshot. Maytubby sniffed hard for tobacco smoke. Nothing but sycamore, which was pleasant but not very helpful. A quarter hour, and they had found no sign. They walked nearer the river, where the bank had been walked by fishermen. A few prints led into the water, but they were from rubber waders.

"Let's find the truck and work from there," he said.

It wasn't far above them, in a clearing. The driver's door was open, the alarm dinging. They both fought the impulse to shut it. Love's bootprints backtracked alongside the unimproved road he had driven. He had bought himself some time. The farther Love followed the road back north, the more likely he would at least have to avoid Eph. Bond cell-phoned the deputy to warn him. Maytubby disliked the idea of Eph confronting Love alone almost as much as he disliked the idea of Hannah doing the same, though for different reasons.

So he was a little relieved when the tracks disappeared on a stone outcrop and did not continue in a straight line on the other side. Love was taking more care now that he was in a foot game. Maytubby and Bond quickly walked the rock's perimeter until Bond found the trail exiting on the river side. As they made their way down, following Love's wafflestompers, they decided Eph should about-face again and meet his ride as planned. Bond could radio Eph because Love had abandoned the pickup.

The last few yards to the river were steep and rocky. Once again they butt-slid down to the water. And once again they each took a bank. Hannah suggested walking south because uncleared land spread farther west of the river that way. They waded south through shallow whitewater toward the hairpin. Maytubby dipped his bandanna in the cold spring water, wiped his face with it, and slid it back on his head. A harrier sailed low over the river, a snake twisting in its talons.

Halfway around the crescent, Bond found the dusty west bank, smudged by Love's wet boots. She tossed a pebble at Maytubby's back. Hunching instinctively, he then turned to follow her. Finding Love's trail, they jogged. Bond's boots sucked and squished. She altered her steps, curled her toes, but nothing worked. At this point, stealth was not likely the main issue. They threaded a mile of rolling woods, sometimes stopping to listen or pick up a lost trail.

They neared the edge of wooded land, which jutted like a peninsula from the river. Love would not expose himself on the prairie. He could only double back.

Just before the crest of a rise, Maytubby stopped and knelt in the underbrush. "I go straight left; you go straight right."

Bond nodded and waded into some brambles. Maytubby went south, moving pretty fast. He danced around a bull snake. It hissed and shook its tail. No sign that Love had passed anywhere.

He was rope-walking a fallen log over a creek bed when a pistol report threw him off balance. He tried a pirouette to get himself going the right way but fell off the log. When he landed, he regretted for an instant not having worn shoes.

He recognized the sound of Hannah's stumpy old Model 10 from the CLEET range. Once out of the creek, Maytubby sprinted until he could hear brush snapping and locate it. Then he veered right and ran even faster, trying to get ahead of the chase. Soon he was, and he wheeled left to get between the commotion and the river.

He found a sturdy buttonbush at the water's edge, stepped up its laddered trunk, and peered through the toxic leaves. He laid his palm on his pistol. Love was coming straight toward him, with Hannah not far behind. At fifty yards, Love's face was pallid and sweat slick. His winded-man grimace showed black teeth.

Maytubby swung down. He hit Love high, and Bond hit him low.

"You … elephant … *cunt!*" Love screamed at Bond, gasping for air.

Hannah's face was smeared with dirt, and blood ran from her nose onto Love's throat. She twisted a sheaf of his greasy hair and held the edge of a stag-handled bowie against his throat. She glared at him and ground her teeth.

She feinted with her elbow, and Love flinched.

"Tongue," she said to Maytubby, though she was staring at Love. "Tongue and gravy and hash browns." Then she tossed the knife at Maytubby's feet. He covered Bond with his pistol, tossed her a set of PlastiCuffs, and recited the warrant and Love's rights while she cuffed his hands and feet and frisked him. She was panting and sweat drenched. Maytubby uncapped his flask, pulled Love to a sitting position, and poured water in his mouth. He swallowed greedily.

While they were catching their wind, Bond and Maytubby sat on boulders, drinking water and keeping an eye on Love, who looked like a corpse left out in the rain. Tossing her head in the direction she and Love had come, she said, "Signal shot, warning shot, whatever. Watch him."

After she disappeared through the possumhaw, he heard her splashing in the river. When she reappeared, her face was clean but for a drop of blood on her upper lip. "He kicked me."

"Resisting arrest, assault on an officer, using the C-word." Maytubby faced Bond and held out the stag bowie on his palm. "Spitting image of the murder weapon, huh? Except this one isn't custom. Company stamp. Silver Stag Pacific Bowie. Could you tell them apart?"

She studied it as she stanched the blood from her nose. "Not on a bet."

To Bond, Maytubby said, "I'm going to cut your hobble." She drew her revolver and trained it on Love while her partner first unbuckled Love's deerskin scabbard and then freed his legs with the Bowie. Maytubby buckled on the scabbard. "You got your camera, Hannah?"

"Left pants pocket."

Maytubby photographed the knife and then sheathed it. After both officers radioed their dispatchers, and the OHP had been notified, Maytubby took Love by the arm and steadied him as they forded the river. Bond followed.

CHAPTER 13

Maytubby had Love booked into Johnston County until Pontotoc County, the closest jail to LHP headquarters, had a free cell the next morning. The nation didn't have its own jail. Since Love had no attorney, Maytubby arranged for a Chickasaw public defender to be at Pontotoc. He called Jill and related the sequel.

In A-OK Pizza on Tishomingo's Main Street, Maytubby finished his third glass of ice water after ordering a side salad and a small sweet pepper and olive pizza. Bond ordered a medium meat lover's and drained a second tumbler of sweet tea. The Landmark Bank sign across the street read 106 at 1:49.

Maytubby dipped a paper napkin in his water glass and beckoned to Bond to lean forward. He wiped dried blood off her upper lip. Until she leaned back in the booth, he had not registered the strange intimacy of the gesture.

He said, "How'd you come to locate and pursue Austin Love before dawn? That's not your shift."

"Couldn't sleep. Can't imagine why. Sheriff lets me take a cruiser if I buy the gas."

"So you've been driving around the county all night on the off chance you'd cross paths, like Ahab trolling the seas for Moby Dick?"

"That bastard preyed on my mind."

Maytubby nodded, watching her spread hands slide slowly back and forth on the tabletop. A plum blotch was spreading over her face.

"I had just made a Uie on 377 at the Pontotoc County line, real close to where I changed Tate's tire. Was almost to Connerville when these headlights approach real fast from behind. That '66 has a big V-8. I would have pursued anyway, but I wouldn't have known it was Love except he passed me in Connerville right where there's that one streetlight in front of the volunteer fire department. Looked like grim Death in a Ford. My radar put him at a hundred and two. Wouldn't pass a cop if he wasn't hopped up. I was afraid I'd lose him before I could goose the Five-Hundred to catch him."

The pizzas arrived, and she started in on hers, giving Maytubby's order a disapproving glance. "He led me a merry chase," she said with her mouth full. "Up and down the paved section roads."

"You see him throw anything out the window?"

"Cigarette butts."

"No cell in the truck or on him. I wonder where he expected to go when he went into the woods."

"Woods better than open prairie. That truck was out of gas."

"True," Maytubby said. "Where could he have been going so fast at that hour? He probably dumped any meth bags he might have had."

"And only two rocks in his pocket. Nothing urgent there."

"Except it's supposed to be really fun to drive fast when you're cranked."

"Least I can sleep tonight." She tore a piece of her pizza in half and held it up as if to propose a toast. "Sleep even better if I'd killed him."

Maytubby ate his salad. A red-faced old man in overalls and no shirt was riding a mule bareback down Main Street. When the mule pulled even with the back of Bond's cruiser, the rider pulled back on the hackamore reins and stopped the mule. Presently, the mule raised its tail and shat on the pavement. Its rider gently urged it on down the street.

Maytubby looked at Bond and raised his brows.

"Alvie Wright. Four DUIs. We have to pay."

"He ever ride under the influence?"

"He ever not?"

They finished their meal in silence. Maytubby paid, and they stood for a moment in the hot shadow of the old brick facade. Bond worked a toothpick with her lips.

"I owe you two, Hannah."

"You could buy me some dry socks."

CHAPTER 14

At headquarters, Sheila gave Maytubby a thumbs-up after buzzing him in the front door. Chief Fox appeared from a suite of window-less offices and congratulated him on Love's capture.

"You know, Bill, you've blown our annual towing budget from the nation." Fox punched him on the shoulder. "*Ada News,* AP, and the *Oklahoman* all left messages. On your desk."

Maytubby walked down a dim corridor and turned into his office. He switched on the fluorescent overhead, casting its anemic blue light on the photo of the nation's governor, who stared back at him with amiable indifference. The little room was stuffy and smelled faintly of mold. Condensation pipes leaked from the ceiling into the walls. He stood in a dank, chilly hole less than three feet from a dazzling inferno he couldn't even see. Every office was more or less the same to him: insufferable.

He leaned on the desk and peeled off sticky notes with reporters' phone numbers. The cross-county pursuit and Love's takedown would make a fetching teaser on the home page, sell some ads for popcorn chicken.

The evidence against Love was strong—so strong that the forensics seemed to Maytubby necessary only because there was no eyewitness. The scientific details would bore a jury already convinced of Love's guilt. But Maytubby didn't feel convinced. He was not altogether sure why. Was Austin Love capable of homicide? Though he certainly didn't mind knocking women around, he didn't seem like a sadist. And he had never stayed with anyone long enough to nurture a dangerous grudge.

The knife bothered him. It would bother him even if the FBI matched the prints. Right by the road, three hundred yards from the crime scene. Love could have tossed it in the Blue—or Lake Texoma, for that matter. There were no knife or gun charges on his sheet. Why would he replace an expensive artisanal knife with a factory version? Quicker way to get a reasonable replica? The mail order would have taken at least a week. But he might have bought it anywhere. It may never even have left its scabbard.

Google yielded websites for thirteen bladesmiths in the region. Maytubby looked at the intent faces of the men at their forges and benches as they crafted their Persian hunters, cowboy fighters, and heart-seekers. Thomas Jefferson had admired those faces—self-reliant, undistorted by the merchant's eagerness to please. Maytubby copied the URLs, made a contacts list called "LoveBowie," and distributed the photo of Love's knife that Hannah had e-mailed him before she returned to the Blue with the sheriff to do her discharged-firearm report. He asked the knife makers if they had recently sold such a knife and, if so, to whom. Had they been asked to copy another knife? If he had to guess, he would say that bladesmiths didn't check their e-mail several times a day, and that a good many knife makers resented having to deal with computers at all. Looking at their spacious work sheds and big windows opening to woods and sky, he felt a little pang of false nostalgia.

To the Associated Press, the beat reporter at the *Ada News,* and the state reporter at the *Oklahoman,* Maytubby related the same story of Love's capture, as sparely as possible. The Johnston County sheriff might contribute more exciting facts. Hannah did not speak to reporters. After her sister was murdered, newspapers had printed her foster father's lies. Maytubby wished the arrest had been routine.

He was not fifteen minutes into the arrest report when his cell phone squawked. "Jake Renaldo" appeared on the screen.

"Hey, Jake."

"Bill. 'Fooz …'—how'd you say that?"

"Bubba."

"Very funny."

"Fusilier. You get the guy driving the Cobalt?"

"No. It was ditched off Hooey Road last night. Tag removed. Tried to torch it but just burned part of a seat. You captured Love, probably scared him."

"Name's Woodley. I think. Anybody see the ditchers?"

"From a long ways away, in the moonlight. Dogs woke the folks up. Dogs got all up on the getaway vehicle. Might be some scratches. One of the dogs got run over and killed. Ditchers left when the car was still burning. Bastards swept off their shoeprints with limbs. No make or model on the vehicle. It drove away lights out. Coal wants to know if LHP wants the Cobalt."

"Yes."

"Pretty soon that gang's gonna run out of vehicles, don'tcha think?"

"Fox says the nation's going to have to sell more letter carts and Bedré truffles to pay our wrecker tab."

"Found some interesting literature in the Cobalt."

"Satan still waitin'?"

"Damn, you're good."

"Hannah stopped this guy Woodley for speeding. Claimed to be a preacher, gave her one of those doomsday leaflets. House on his license in Tushka's been vacant for years. Same flyers blew out of a small light-colored car I was pursuing east of Antlers. Probably him. Found a place down there I think he and maybe Love and others were living. Nobody home. Probably won't be anymore."

"You're taking the Cobalt so you can get the preacher for accessory after?"

"I don't know."

Early in the evening, Maytubby finished his arrest report. He checked his e-mail. Not a single knife maker had responded.

CHAPTER 15

Maytubby banged and tugged on the double-hung windows in his old house to get them open. He would switch on the three window units next, but right now he had to get some fresh air inside. When the indoor temperature broke ninety-five, he finally went for it: refrigerated air. This evening, it was 105. All his AC units had to be tiny because the wiring had been added to the house the same year as the bathroom—1932—and had never been updated. He hoarded fuses.

The territorial gable-and-wing perched on the bank of an old Katy railroad cut—now a bike path that ran very near Jill Milton's neighborhood. The rent was cheap, the climate uncontrollable. Most days, wind whistled through fissures and holes. In the dead of winter, with every sash nestled in its frame, his panel curtains danced as if on a spring breeze. Naked light bulbs hung on long, twisted wires from the high ceilings. The water that issued from squeaky taps into the chipped enamel basins was often rusty.

Still, the house was clean and spare and sunny. It had spiritual room, and its heat and cold and drafts, Maytubby believed, raised his threshold of discomfort. Jill Milton was happy with her threshold of discomfort. She also preferred her shower to a claw-foot tub and a plastic beer mug.

He switched on a box fan and pulled down the long chrome handle of his 1950s Frigidaire. On the door, Jill had penciled four boxes with a cherry in each, above the word JACKPOT. He took out a red metal pitcher of water, a honeydew melon, an avocado, and a lime and set them all on the counter. He poured a glass of water. Then he sliced the melon and the avocado, halved the lime, and squeezed it over them. Under his arm, he tucked the Modern Library Classics edition of *Selected Poems of Emily Dickinson*, edited by the poet Billy Collins. Under the canopy of a mature pecan tree, Maytubby laid out his "tea," as Jill called his early last meal of the day, on an old school desk. He slid into the seat and opened the book at random, excited. She could do *Twilight Zone* better than Rod Serling. Give you gooseflesh.

His white-over-bronze 1965 Ford pickup, recently tuned up and outfitted with new tires, sat under the pecan, covered with tree litter. No joggers or cyclists came along the path. The air was still, not a bird singing. Sugar ants matted the plate he had laid on the dead grass. His vegetable garden had been broiled to a crisp, all but the okra. Its thick stalks were still a vibrant green and putting on fruit above Maytubby's reach. Like the medieval Egyptians, he chopped it up, rolled it in meal, and fried it.

Maytubby went back to the Frigidaire four times for cold water. At dusk, he called Jill Milton. "Earl Scruggs," she said.

"You know how you can tell one banjo tune from another?"

"They have different names. That's old."

"I just heard it this week on Rodeo Opry."

"On the radio in the turnip truck?"

"Yep. Same station that plays Stephen Foster songs."

"Watch it, buster."

"I'm reading an upright Yankee, Emily Dickinson, while you're wallowing in Confederate nostalgia."

"I doubt your rebel ancestors marched against the Union Indians to Bach's Invention Eight."

"The medium is the message, Miss Milton."

"On the other hand, lots of Emily Dickinson poems could be sung to 'Oh! Susanna.'"

"And to the theme of *Gilligan's Island*. That proves nothing." Maytubby fanned himself with the classifieds section of the *Ada News*.

"You want me to be the good cop at your interrogation tomorrow?"

"You're not a cop."

"I could put on a uniform and bring him candy bars and tell you to lay off it."

"I want to be the good cop."

"So who's going to be the bad cop?"

"I'm working on it, but you do have to be a real cop to be a bad cop."

"Naomi Colbert doing PD for Love?"

"She is."

"The nation will elect her to the supreme court someday."

"I hope so."

"Will Love talk at all?"

"Silence is all we dread."

"You bringing him to Pontotoc early?"

"Yep. Where are you?"

"The city. Grant summit at the capitol."

"Plant a flag for me."

CHAPTER 16

Naomi Colbert held a Ticonderoga pencil eraser-down on the interrogation table. She spread her other hand over a canary legal pad. A slight overbite made her appear to be smiling, but she was not. Maytubby had given her all the information he had on the case. Austin Love sat on her left at the square table. He wore orange prison scrubs, and he stank. Probably jonesing. He ignored the Styrofoam cup of coffee in front of him and stared at the wall.

Maytubby came into the room with three bananas. "Mr. Love knows the rules, Ms. Colbert?"

"He does."

Maytubby said, "Mr. Love, the same day that Majesty Tate was stabbed and killed, four witnesses saw you together at the Lazy K in Sulphur. They said you and she hugged and kissed. Several people in Bromide saw your truck coming and going on the road leading to Majesty Tate's rented house for a couple of days before the murder and on the day of the murder. The FBI and the LHP have matched the tire prints in her yard to the tires on your pickup. In the bar ditch on that road, I found a bloody stag-handled Bowie resembling the knife you always carried in a leg scabbard. You siphoned gas from your uncle's truck the night of the murder. And you fled from officers of three law enforcement agencies. These are all facts. Do you want to dispute them?"

Love stared at the wall over Maytubby's right shoulder.

"Did you stab Majesty Tate?"

He didn't take his eyes from the wall. "No."

"Did you have a sexual relationship with her?"

Love's eyes shifted slightly, and his face loosened. He was thinking this over.

"You don't have to answer," Colbert reminded him.

"Yeah," Love said, staring at the wall. Colbert frowned and wrote something on her pad.

"Did you ever hit her?"

Colbert repeated her caution to Love. He said nothing.

"On the evening of the murder, when did you leave Tate's house?"

Silence.

"Did she say that she was afraid of anyone?"

Nothing.

"When did you learn that Tate had been murdered?"

Somewhere in the building, a cell clanged shut.

"If you didn't kill Tate, why did you run?"

Love was still as a tiki.

"Did the knife found near Bromide after Tate's murder belong to you?"

"No."

"Dave Woodley try to win you to Jesus?"

Love's eyes widened a wee bit, and the edges of his lips moved. Maytubby had scored a palpable hit.

"Does Woodley talk funny? Does he say 'wahn' instead of 'wine'?"

"I don't know what you're talking about," Love growled.

"He picked you up after you abandoned your truck at Kullihoma."

Back to the stony gaze.

"The Cobalt was ditched yesterday. They—Woodley and friends, I'm guessing—tried to burn it. Any idea what that was about?"

Maytubby thought he saw Love's embouchure contract toward "no," but he said nothing, possibly recalling that silence and denial were not the same.

"Wiley Bates riding with your outfit again?"

A toilet flushed somewhere in the jail. The supply pipe rattled loudly.

"He just moved out of his place in Coalgate and took that fancy new bass boat with him." Maytubby watched the muscles around the fixed eyes. Some evanescent motion, but not a palpable hit.

"I bet the Antlers Hilton was quiet last night." Maytubby peeled and ate half a banana. He could be quiet, too. And was, for a space of ten minutes. Naomi Colbert tapped her pencil eraser quietly on her legal pad. "I think all your coyotes've left you with your leg in the trap."

Love sat motionless.

Maytubby wondered whether Colbert had told her client she had a court date in thirty minutes. Soon find out. He ate the second and third bananas and threw the peels in the trash. "One of your coyotes killed Majesty Tate and you don't help us, you're going to be a seventy-year-old prison rodeo clown."

Twenty-five minutes passed in silence. Love never looked at Colbert's watch. She hadn't told him. Maytubby and Colbert rose at the same time, and a Pontotoc deputy took Love back to his cell.

When Maytubby returned to headquarters, a tow truck was depositing the Cobalt next to Love's monster truck. He looked at the Bubba Fusilier dealer sticker. The VIN numbers were intact, but Woodley had taken the tag. Maybe he thought nobody was paying him any attention, that the Coal sheriff would dump it on the auction lot and forget about it.

There was one new post in his Chickasaw.net e-mail. It was

from Grover Jessup, "the Knife Wizard." The subject line read, "Knife." The message read, "I will talk to you about the knife. No e-mails. Park behind my workshop." A Google map for the site included a sharp aerial photograph of Jessup's workshop, which was near Byrds Prairie Cemetery, south of Tupelo. Maytubby was there in twenty-five minutes.

Jessup switched off his bellows and pulled his sweat-stained leather apron over his head. "I been goin' after it hammer and tongs," he said with a little grin.

Maytubby laughed, knowing that old Grover had to make the same crack to every stranger.

"Have a seat."

Jessup moved a pedestal fan closer to the chairs. In a small, brightly lit display case, a dozen knives glittered. Their handles were inlaid with turquoise, mother-of-pearl, and copper.

"This is about that girl over in Bromide, isn't it?" Jessup said.

"Yes, it is. We have reason to suspect that knife may have been the murder weapon."

"I hope not."

"Because you made it?"

"Yessir," Jessup said, pulling a copy of the photo from his shirt pocket. He opened it and pointed to a little dot on the hilt. "I'm going to get another Bowie from the case." Holding the knife out handle-first, Jessup tapped his finger on a tiny "J" stamped on the hilt.

Maytubby nodded. "Did you make the knife in the picture for someone recently?"

"Yes and no. Fella from around Krebs brought in a chunk of antler from a buck he shot last fall. That was about a month ago. Paid me half to make the knife, then called back two weeks ago to say he had to make child support and wouldn't finish paying for it. I laid it on the counter by the case, was going to polish it up for display. Wasn't too long after that a fella drove up in some little old green Toyota, from the nineties maybe. Come in, in a big hurry, didn't say 'boo.' Had on a baseball cap and wraparound sunglasses.

He went to the display, looked at my stock for all of three seconds, then half turned around. The Bowie on the counter caught his eye. He unsheathed it, put his elbow on the counter, and the butt of the knife next to it. Seemed to be measuring. Sheathed the knife and nodded at me. I said three-fifty, and he said three, like a question. I nodded back and he gave me six fifties. He left in a big hurry."

"You see his hair color?"

"It wasn't dark. Hair on his arm was pale."

Maytubby established that the buyer was white, of medium build and height. He wore jeans, brown chukkas, light-blue T-shirt, and a black baseball cap. When Maytubby asked if the cap had printing on it, Jessup wrinkled his nose and pointed his finger at him. "Something funny. Toad suck."

"State park in Arkansas. You see the tag on his car?" Maytubby showed Jessup photos of Tercels.

"No, I didn't. It's that one," he pointed to a 1995 coupe.

Maytubby handed Jessup a card. "You make beautiful knives with your hammer and tongs, sir. Give me a call if you think of any detail that comes to mind."

Preliminary reports from both the medical examiner and FBI forensics were in his e-mail when he returned to headquarters. Majesty Tate's death had been ruled a homicide. She had been killed by multiple stab wounds to the heart and neck. Her blood was on the knife Maytubby found, but the killer had worn latex gloves. Tate had had sexual intercourse during the twenty-four hours before her murder, and DNA taken from residual semen was a close match to Austin Love's profile in the offender DNA database. DNA taken from skin and body hair under Tate's fingernails did not match Love's, but it did match one other sample in the CODIS national database, from an unsolved Arkansas murder.

Maytubby called Naomi Colbert, related the exculpatory evidence, and forwarded the report. He also called the Chickasaw National District Court. Love had been smart not to lie about having sex with Tate. He still might be a material witness, and he had some serious parole issues. Not going anywhere tonight. Maytubby knew that he knew a lot. And also that he didn't know everything, or he wouldn't be in Pontotoc.

Also in his box was a post from the regional Bureau of Indian Affairs office in Ada, copied to all enforcement offices connected to the Tate case. According to BIA property records, the house Majesty Tate rented, though it sat in the center of forty acres of old tribal allotment land, was not, in fact, on tribal land. When it was built, the lending bank would not issue a mortgage if it remained on tribal land, out of the bank's reach. Maytubby stared at the blue screen.

CHAPTER 17

Jill Milton strained some tortellini from her soup and held the spoon out to Maytubby. "Yes?"

He bit them off the spoon. "Yes."

She was wearing a periwinkle cotton camp shirt very well. Mozart's second horn concerto was playing softly in Gjorgjo's on Ada's Main Street. A votive flickered through their glasses of old-vine red. Maytubby wore a khaki twill oxford shirt—a little faded but pressed to an edge. He raised his glass. "To square one," he said. They clinked glasses. "These mussels really are good."

"Yessir."

"And your grantspersonship?"

"Matched only by my keen evasion skills. The capitol facade was shedding chunks of masonry like that." She pointed to the half loaf of bread on the table. "I put my laptop on my head."

"Harrowing."

"Oh, it got much worse at the summit. The forces of green split peas clashed with the forces of yellow split peas. The pinto contingent struck them both. No party wanted to settle for a round third of the half ton budgeted in that line."

"I didn't know that bean varieties awakened such passions."

"That's because you live in an ivory tower. You're out of touch with the real world."

She bumped his knee under the table and gave him a fine smile. He wanted to be with her forever.

"So that little reservation you had about Love being a major thug—it was justified," she said, starting on her soup.

He stared at her until she tapped on the table. "Earth to Bill."

"What?" He cradled her elbow with his sunburnt hand.

"You weren't sure Love killed Majesty Tate."

He cleared his throat. "I was hoping I was wrong. Now that an Indian is no longer a suspect, the case would go to the feds. I learned from the BIA today that Tate's house is not on allotment land, even though the forty acres around it are tribal. So the case goes to local and state. OSBI will be the main player."

"But you'll still be involved."

"As much as the state wants me to be. Hannah and I know the most about it." Mozart's bouncy third movement ended. Pans clanked back in the kitchen.

"Have you been reimagining the murder while you were chasing Love?"

"I've wondered how all these shadowy players fit into the guy's life. Now would be a good time to find out."

"So you think one of them is the culprit."

"Well, yeah." He wagged his head. "I've done all this *work*."

"You're counting out a rogue?"

"The chances of a rogue killing Majesty Tate with a knife exactly like Austin Love's are slim, I would say."

"Unless that person is not a rogue but you're discounting him because you haven't run into him yet."

"True."

"But that's too discouraging to think about."

"Way."

"You think when Love learns he's no longer a suspect, he'll help you?"

"Not by telling me anything. If he hadn't resisted, he'd be blasting around those county roads, trying to find the guy who tried to frame him. Doing my work for me."

"Wouldn't you run the risk of losing him?"

"I have a vast network of informants."

"Yeah? Name one."

"You see that guy over my left shoulder, sitting at the bar?"

"The blond one with the mullet and the Hawaiian shirt?"

Maytubby raised one brow and nodded gravely.

"So who does he snitch on: hair stylists and Parrotheads?"

"Nutritionists. You see how he sticks to you, and you don't notice him?"

"Yeah, I see." She drank a little wine and set her glass down. "Who will the state send down?"

"My guess is, Dan Scrooby." Maytubby twirled a tortellini in his red sauce and ate it.

"Where have I heard that name?"

A middle-aged couple entered the restaurant, a gust of hot wind in their wake. The votives flickered.

"It's the English village the Pilgrims left. The Scrooby separatists."

"Oh, yeah. I think I forget it because I want it to be someplace with a fancier name."

"Like Barking."

"Like Shitterton. What's he like?"

"Sighs a lot. Puckers up before he exhales. You know, exasperated. He doesn't suffer fools gladly."

"Sounds like he found the perfect job."

"Actually, he did. He would be depressed if he couldn't feel aggrieved."

"Would you like another detective better?"

"He's okay."

"That's what you said about Katz."

"I have to guard against becoming terminally aggrieved."

"Mm-hm."

He drained the carafe into her glass. She swirled the wine around and watched it slowly rappel down the sides.

"Has Sol Stoddard returned to frighten the children with his family values?"

"No. I read in the *Tulsa World* he's going to formally announce his candidacy for governor of Oklahoma next week."

"Still curious if it was his Lexus Hannah saw parked at Boggy Depot beside the notorious Cobalt. She thought the two guys were hooking up."

"That would make for a lively campaign revelation." "Yes, it would. I need a pretext to search it."

The temperature was still over a hundred as they walked the few blocks to the McSwain Theater, newly restored by the Chickasaw Nation, to watch *Pearl*, a nation-funded film about Pearl Carter, a very young Chickasaw pilot in the 1920s.

"We'll see what they did without us," Maytubby said as they entered the cold lobby.

They both had been asked to audition as extras, and both were told the same thing when they were not cast: "Your face is too striking. You'll distract the audience." They believed it and didn't believe it, each for different reasons.

The film had been out a while, but they hadn't seen it. As they left the theater, Maytubby said, "Films about child prodigies always make me feel not quite up to snuff."

"You're a pilot."

"I wasn't a twelve-year-old pilot—or a teenage barnstormer."

"You should be worrying about the famous aviator Wiley Post. His eye patch was hot."

"Hotter than my barbed-wire fence scar?"

"A thousand times."

"You think there are any after-hours eye patch stores in Ada?"

CHAPTER 18

Oklahoma State Bureau of Investigation Agent Dan Scrooby sat in one of the plastic booths at the Ada Travel Center. He was wearing khaki pants, a navy polo shirt with the OSBI star embroidered on the chest, and a Heckler & Koch P30 in a Texas cross-draw belt holster. He stared at a laptop screen as he ate a sausage biscuit from the buffet. Behind him, a skinny young man in a Chickasaw Nation security guard uniform stood at the door between the travel shop and its casino. When a casino patron entered or left, the trills and bings promising good fortune, along with a cloud of tobacco smoke, wafted into the shop.

Maytubby slid into the booth and faced Scrooby, who did not look up from the screen when he said "Bill." He exhaled loudly and shook his head. "Where do they get these people?"

"Dan. Where do who get *what* people?"

Scrooby scowled at the screen and jabbed a finger at it. "*These* people."

"Oh, yeah. You're right. They are an epic pain in the ass."

"You got that right." Scrooby slapped down the screen of his laptop and pushed it aside. His face shone with sweat. "So, looks like your ex-con meth cooker was set up. I tried to talk to him this morning. You know where that got me. Perp's likely Anglo, wouldn't you say?"

"Chances are. That's why you're here."

Scrooby lifted a clipboard from the booth seat—police media were still migrating from the old ways—laid it on the table, and started flipping through completed forms and printed e-mail exchanges. He stopped near the bottom. "This car burning—it speak to you?"

"Yeah. It says if the arsonist was stupid, he didn't bring enough accelerant, and if the arsonist was cunning, he brought just enough."

"To preserve evidence incriminating …?"

"The owner, maybe."

Scrooby flipped a couple of pages on the clipboard. "The nonpreacher preacher Woodley, who is a nonresident in the residence listed on his registration."

"And he could have done it himself."

At this, the agent finally looked up. "To incriminate himself?"

"I'm not sure he is himself."

Scrooby nodded as he took a shark bite out of his sausage biscuit. "If this guy is not a preacher, doesn't live where he says he does, and owns the car Love used to elude pursuit for a crime he didn't commit, what's he doing around here?"

"He might have known Love was seeing Tate. He might have bought the lookalike knife. He might have killed Tate. No prints, but you've got the DNA from her nails. Might match some hair or something left in the Cobalt. Red hair isn't hard to spot. That Cobalt has a Louisiana dealer sticker on it. The CODIS DNA match was an Arkansas murder. Arkansas is between here and there. The Arkansas murder weapon was a Winchester thirty-thirty rifle. Common deer gun. Killer at least fifty yards away—basically a sniper. Victim was in a property dispute with a powerful real estate broker."

"We can do the hair. You're saying maybe hired gun? But why would this guy go to all this trouble when he could kill Tate the same way and disappear?"

"Maybe he didn't want to establish a pattern. Maybe he was

making things interesting. Maybe the other case also had a fall guy but with different habits."

"Who hired him to kill Tate?"

"I don't know. The only thing I have now is that Deputy Hannah Bond, in Johnston, saw Woodley park next to a white Lexus, no tag ID, in a dark corner of Boggy Depot. Woodley got in the Lexus. Hannah left because she thought they were just hooking up. My girlfriend knows that Solomon Stoddard drives a new white Lexus ES."

Scrooby exhaled in almost a whistle. "I think I saw the presidential limousine parked in the Wayne cemetery yesterday." He looked at the ceiling. "Besides …" He scooted his laptop toward himself, pushing the clipboard aside. He typed a few dozen characters and swiveled the computer around so Maytubby could view Stoddard's record in every crime database up to the National Crime Information Center. Maytubby toured the sites. At one, he memorized Stoddard's plate: 43X-3827. He turned the computer around.

"Not even a parking ticket. Wife's a stone fox, too." Scrooby snapped the laptop shut for emphasis. "Sol gets in, he's promised law enforcement more officers and big raises."

"You have most of the facts," Maytubby said. "How can I help you?"

"I'm closer to the city. Let me see if I can find out what Tate was doing up there."

"I'll look into that Arkansas case and try to find Woodley."

Scrooby had already opened his laptop. He nodded but didn't look up. Before Maytubby had reached the exit, he heard Scrooby sigh.

CHAPTER 19

By concealing her patrol car more cunningly and lowering her tolerance slightly, Hannah Bond managed a good morning's take in only two hours. As her last citation drove slowly away, she followed the car on State 7 and then turned north into Bromide. She followed Main Street out of town (and out of Johnston County), watching for a jeep track that the Web map said should be splitting off to her left. It soon appeared, and she took it.

Her book of moving violations wouldn't be worth the pain and suffering if she whacked a muffler, so she drove gingerly up into the scrubby woods spreading several miles behind the house where Majesty Tate was murdered. Veils of white dust rose on thermals above the quarries to the west. Because evidence was plentiful on the south side of the hill, she and Maytubby had ignored the woods behind the house, on the north side.

Though the blue grama grass between the ruts had gone dormant in the drought, it was almost as tall as the roadside grass and didn't appear to be broken. Bond kept moving so her exhaust pipes wouldn't sit long enough to kindle a prairie fire. When the track crossed a barren dry wash, she turned off the cruiser and walked it. She found only a couple of truck treads where the track crossed the wash—so old they were set in mud. To the east, nothing in the sand but coon and deer prints, snake waves. A buzzard's shadow flicked across the rocks.

About a hundred yards west of the road, she found herself looking down at two sets of dirt bike tracks, a little smudged by wind. Near the grass line, the tracks were a little sharper. She took a calendar card from her pocket and laid the ruler side across the tread print, photographed them with her phone. Both front and back tires were four inches wide. Bond knew they were from one bike—the front with spiked tread blocks and the rear with widely spaced paddle-shaped tread blocks. And she knew that these treads were for riding in sand.

On the margins of the wash, where the tracks came and went, she could find grass stems broken by the bike, but she couldn't follow the trail more than a few feet. Back in the cruiser, she crept back into the thatch of dusty oak and red cedar as she climbed toward the crest. On her laptop, she watched her progress, satellites in black space guiding her toward the crooked hall-and-parlor house.

The track ended shy of the hilltop, not far from a small clearing where there was a spring. The spring did not have a name on the map. Bond could see a camouflaged deer stand twenty yards off the road. That explained the track, which followed no fences and led to no house or petroleum well. The last of the manifold deer seasons, from black powder to crossbow, had ended six months ago. It was unlikely that out-of-season hunters would use an established camp so near a town. Besides, those hunters would be in pickups or on four-wheelers.

Bond walked shrinking circles around the camp and into the clearing but saw no more bike tracks. She climbed the ladder into the stand, found nothing there but a few empty Evan Williams pints and two 30.06 shell casings. The hall-and-parlor house was no more than a half mile downhill from the camp. Though the grade was gentle, Bond switchbacked, checking cattle trails for prints, looking for places a slipping bike tire might have scuffed. She flushed a roadrunner, and the rustle sent her hand to her pistol grip. The bird sped off in its ducking-chicken-pedaling-a-bicycle way.

By the time the crooked roof appeared through a crosshatch of oak limbs, Bond had spent the margin the speed trap had bought her. And she was more than a half mile from her cruiser. She wrung the sweat from her baseball cap and drank from her canteen. Then she walked fast around the yard and behind the house, searching for bike tracks. The only prints anywhere near the house, except for hers and Tate's and Maytubby's, had been the Survivor boots that Love wore. Three minutes and nothing. She gauged the area where someone could stand and see everything going on in the house through the double rear windows, and then she walked it, back and forth, turning over leaves and twigs and downed branches. She felt a little surge of anger at Love's exoneration—at the real killer's invisibility. It was hard for her to retrain her imagination.

The sunlight caught a little flash. She saw a small disk of creased foil that trailed a paper scrap marked with a pastel green T. She photographed it. From her utility belt, she took a latex glove and a baggie, then picked up the swatch of Tums wrapper and sealed it away. The wrapper hadn't seen the weather of six months, but then again, this was Oklahoma—it might have blown here from Saskatchewan. Not ten feet up the hill, she found a Survivor boot print pointing toward the house. A little depression next to it looked like a knee print. She laid the ruler across both and photographed them.

Then she covered ground swiftly with her Paul Bunyan stride. Inside fifteen minutes, she was passing an Amish buggy on Bromide Road. The dispatcher in Tish was mercifully silent. Parking where Maytubby had found the knife, she walked up the road toward the front side of the house. Even through the polarized aviator sunglasses, the dust was dazzling.

Before she was halfway to the crooked house, she saw, between many other tire prints, the narrow checkered prints of dirt bike tires. She laid her ruler across one and photographed it. She had no time to go further, and she was low on water.

Rounding the last bend, she saw the sheriff's cruiser parked in front of hers. Sheriff Benny Magaw was leaning into the rearview mirror, combing his few wisps of dyed hair. He rolled the window down and smiled at her.

"Deputy."

"Sheriff."

"Catch a lot of speeders on this stretch, do you?"

She waited.

"Love is in jail, Hannah. OSBI'll do a good job. I need you doing the county's work."

Bond nodded and touched her hat brim with two fingers, turned toward her cruiser.

"Taxpayers don't want to pay twice for the same service," Magaw said to her back.

She frowned as she pulled around the sheriff's cruiser. Then, instead of making a bootleg turn to head back toward Bromide, she drove around the bend, toward the crooked house. Magaw would not know whether to follow her or wait for her. She smiled. Just beyond the bend, she slewed into the bar ditch, made a tight U-turn, and kicked back down the road. Magaw was just rounding the bend when she blew past him. His cruiser disappeared behind a veil of dust.

Beside US 377, near where she changed Majesty Tate's flat, Bond parked in the shade of a burr oak and adjusted her radar. She waved at a few pickups when they honked at her. Her cell rang. No contact name appeared, so she said, "Deputy Bond."

"This is Aaron Coblentz, Deputy Bond." She could hear a calf bawling and remembered that his phone was in his barn so it would not disturb his household. A sensible Amish custom.

"Yes, Mr. Coblentz."

"You said to call if I remembered another strange vehicle around Bromide." He paused. "I did. Going back to Clarita on Limestone Road, I met a motorcycle coming the other way, toward Clarita. One funny thing about it was that it was tall and skinny and had fenders that were very high above the wheels. The other funny thing was its color. It was the color of sand. Not red sand like in the rest of the state. *Sand* sand. And the driver's helmet and shirt were the same color."

"Could you tell if the driver was male or female?"

"Male."

"How fast was he going?"

"Not fast."

"Could you make out the driver's complexion or hair color?"

"He was white. That's all I know. Not really short or tall."

"Would you mind if I stopped by later and showed you some photos of motorcycles?"

After Bond's shift—a lucrative one for Johnston County—Coblentz identified the camo dirt bike as a late-model Suzuki RM-Z250. A few searches, and she found the tire whose front tread she had photographed: a Dunlop MX 71 Geomax Hard Terrain.

When she phoned Maytubby, he was driving through Tupelo, just a few miles away, so they met in the middle. She offered to drive the Tums wrapper to OSBI Purcell, and she told him about the dirt bike and Survivor prints and what she had learned from Coblentz. She had e-mailed him the print photos, which he would forward to OSBI.

"Magaw cutting you slack to work for OSBI?"

"Hell, no. He found me up at the Tate house and got his tail up in the air about it. *Huh!* I went back to my speed trap in a big hurry." She lowered her eyelids conspiratorially. "Gave him a dust bath."

Maytubby smiled. "I'm headed to Love's old hangout in Antlers. Then over to Hope, Arkansas, to talk to the State CID about the murder with the DNA matching Tate's killer's. On down to south Louisiana—see what I can dig up on our favorite man of the cloth."

"Bring me back some tasso."

"I can do that."

When Maytubby saw the elk skull with hot lips, there was just enough light left to illuminate the tracks of a dirt bike, if any were there to find. He parked in the road and once again walked along the drive. Since he had been there, one or two big trucks had used it. Topping a rise, he looked down on a pile of charred lumber, squared in by a blackened chain-wall foundation. Unlike the Cobalt, this house was annihilated. The debris stank. It was a recent fire. Next to the house was a red Chevy pickup, its passenger side scorched, the mirror and molding melted like candle wax. And hitched to the back, an eerily warped Bass Tracker, its big Merc outboard split from its mount and lying on the sand like a dead ape. The Pushmataha sheriff's deputy he had talked to must have forgotten Maytubby's call.

He walked around the pickup to the unfired side. The paint on passenger door was scored all over. Firefighters had scrambled the yard. He found no motorcycle prints there or on the driveway. He started the cruiser, then killed it and walked toward the road's dead end, near the bank of the Kiamichi.

It was deep dusk in the river brush, so he switched on his Maglite and followed the circular turnabout until a little path— maybe a game path, or at most a fishing trail—opened toward the river. Bending over the sand, he moved very slowly, playing his light in a zigzag across the path. A bullfrog jug-a-rummed below. The path angled down until it merged with one that ran along the river. Maytubby turned left, upriver.

He found the knobby tread quickly. It veered off the path, away from the river. He laid his ruler across it and photographed it, recording its GPS location for OSBI. A patch of brittle cattails had been flattened. He knelt and searched the root line carefully. Nothing but toads and mosquitoes. He walked directly toward the burned house, through heavy brush, looking for signs left by the cycle rider, who may have been carrying accelerant. Considering the house, a single match could have done the job. Maytubby couldn't find even one broken limb. And returning to the river, he found no containers that had not held beer or bait.

He phoned Scrooby at home.

"I'm having spareribs with my lovely wife, Sergeant Maytubby."

"I'm in Antlers. Was Wiley Bates in that pile of charcoal I just looked at?"

"Pushmataha called us."

"Why didn't you call me?"

Scrooby exhaled heavily into his phone. "Sergeant, I am overworked. I cannot possibly remember every name on every prayer chain. Also, I am off duty, and I am hungry. Good night."

Maytubby e-mailed Scrooby what he had found, and attached the print photos. He called Jill Milton and wished her a good night. She was still at a meeting of her book club. They had read *Angle of Repose* by Wallace Stegner. He was reading it, too, but he stayed out of her book club because he liked the other one better, the one with just the two of them.

He did not relish three hours of empty two-lane blacktop through the Ouachita. Even so, he didn't drive fast. The country was teeming with deer.

The night was hot. A three-quarter moon etched the highest ridges of Blackjack Mountain. Insects popped like hail on his windshield. Did Woodley burn his car and take to the dirt bike? Had he always ridden the bike? Was he the driver of the green Tercel, who bought the stag Bowie? Did he frame Love? What was Bates doing at the Antlers house? Was he incinerated to shut him up? Or did he just get drunk and knock over a kerosene lamp? Maybe he drank enough Heaven Hill to spontaneously combust.

The little towns came and went: North Pole, Steel Junction, Tiner—some without a single streetlamp. On its newer stretches, US 70 bypassed towns and took a straighter path through the low mountains than its predecessors. Pines crowded the right-of-way and threw jagged moon shadows across the asphalt.

Only a logging truck every dozen miles or so broke the road's monotony. The closest NPR station, KTXK in Texarkana, waxed and waned as the cruiser topped a ridge or dropped into a swale. The Cleveland Symphony was playing Schubert, a composer Maytubby disliked, but not nearly as much as he disliked Christian rock with its mindless repetition and gooey tunes. Country, well … The Schubert faded, and Maytubby turned the radio off. The road slowly unwound.

He had just passed the Eagletown turnoff, not far from the state line, when he heard a snap. A chip appeared in the windshield. His mind was just making the leap from gravel to bullet when a rising shriek silenced the road noise. A ghostly form appeared at the passenger window, backlit by the moon. Its head, reflecting the cruiser's orange dash lights, warped into a smile. Maytubby's skin burned. He stomped the brake and saw the muzzle flash of a very long pistol just beyond his windshield. Before the biker could brake, Maytubby pulled behind him and accelerated. The biker could not turn around with the pistol, and Maytubby checked him when he veered left or right. There was no tag on the bike, and its lights were out. The Amish man's description was perfect: sand-colored helmet, suit, gloves, and boots.

Again the banshee scream as the cyclist leaned into full throttle. The Charger fell behind for a few seconds. The motorcyclist turned on his lights and disappeared around a bend as Maytubby accelerated past the dirt bike's top speed.

Beyond the bend, the road was empty. Maytubby rolled down his window and slowed, listening to the snarl and searching each of the tracks that peeled off the highway. At last, he saw the ruby taillight bobbing north up a steep hillside just before the bike went airborne and vanished over the crest.

North of the highway lay the rugged forests of the southern Ouachita, webbed with thousands of unnamed and unnumbered roads. The next state highway was thirty miles north, the direction the bike had gone. Maytubby would just have to wait until the day that fellow decided to show himself again.

At an abandoned roadhouse, the only structure in Ultima Thule, he pulled onto an apron, turned off his lights, opened the door, and listened for the two-stroke engine. First some coyotes yowling, then the little chain-saw snarl, far back in the hills. He switched on his cabin light, looked at the hole in the back window, and fingered the exit hole in the front. Likely a .357 Magnum.

As he crossed the state line, Maytubby reported the shooting to OHP, then called the Pontotoc sheriff's office and warned the dispatcher that Austin Love's life might be in danger. Scrooby would be sleeping off his ribs.

The country flattened a little, but the road was unfamiliar. At De Queen, Maytubby decided he was within striking distance of Hope. A sleepy night clerk at Clock Inn slid a room key into a little drawer and shoved it at him. A sheet of cracked Plexiglas with a hole in the middle covered the drawer. A sign on it said "Stick Finger in Hole and Yank." Maytubby did as instructed. He parked the cruiser out of view of the street. He fell asleep fast but was awakened after midnight by a dirt bike screaming down US 71. It continued down the highway, as did the one a half hour after that, and the one another fifteen minutes later. De Queen apparently held great allure for nocturnal dirt bikers. He should have driven on to Hope. Who would stoop so low as to break the peace of Hope?

The Southwest Regional HQ of the Arkansas State Police CID occupied the latest in economical and low-maintenance public building designs, its steeply pitched roof a nod to the fashion in new tract homes. But the roof was metal, and it was blue. At seven thirty, Lieutenant Lynn Washington swung into the parking lot just behind Maytubby. As they shook hands, Washington noticed the hole in the windshield.

"Last night," Maytubby said.

"No shit."

"Don't worry. Oklahoma side of the line."

"You think it was my shooter?"

"I don't know."

There was nothing on Washington's desk but a telephone and a small closed laptop. The room was immaculate—not even a paper clip or a crumb on the carpet. A matted and framed diploma from the University of Arkansas said that Washington had earned a BS degree in criminal justice and that he had earned it magna cum laude.

He reached into a desk drawer, pulled out a manila folder, and slid it toward Maytubby. "Have a seat. You want coffee?"

"No thanks." Maytubby picked up the folder. "How did you get DNA from a sniper?"

"One of his ejected shells fell next to a honey locust trunk."

"Ouch."

"Yes. He apparently tried but failed to recover it. Or maybe he just didn't see the thorns in the dark—they're black."

"And long. And the *thorns* have thorns."

"You see we found a scrap of Tums wrapper."

Maytubby flipped through the material in the folder. He stopped when he read that a suspect was interrogated and released. He pointed to the page. "Why was this Boone questioned?"

"He's an itinerant roofer. He'd roofed an outbuilding for the victim. Some people saw them arguing in Arkadelphia about money."

"Same DNA cleared Boone and my suspect."

"Yes sir."

"And what happened to the other party in the roofing dispute?"

"He won."

"You suspect him of hiring a hit?"

"I questioned him and looked around pretty thoroughly. Got a warrant and looked through his phone records, bank records, e-mails. If he hired a hit, he did it far from here and with cash from somewhere else."

"Do you know if he had any southern Louisiana connections— or went there often?"

"I didn't find anything that would make me think that."

"Did you find any motorcycle tread prints near the shooter's position?"

"Nothing. There was a paved county road nearby. Usually deserted. He could have parked on it or had someone waiting for him. We hit dead ends in every direction. Hell, there wasn't even a mysterious stranger in town."

"Did you find any shoe prints?"

Washington jabbed an index finger at the wall. "Oh, yeah. That's the other reason we questioned Boone. He wore Red Wing Wellington boots with crepe wedge soles, and so did the shooter."

"Really." Maytubby told Washington about the Survivor boots in Bromide.

"Now we got DNA *and* fall guys," Washington said. "I think I'll find whatever roof Boone is shingling this week, climb up there, and ask him a few more questions."

"Wait till he gets to a shady part."

"Hey, I went to policeman school, too."

CHAPTER 20

The heat was no respecter of state lines. As Maytubby passed through El Dorado, a bank thermometer missing a few teeth read 97 at 11:00 a.m. He checked his mirrors for a sandman on a skinny bike.

There was no quick route to Jennings, Louisiana, for which Maytubby was grateful. He was so sleepy, an hour on an interstate would have done him in. His Web map said he would spend about ten minutes on I-49, the rest of his trip winding through the Kisatchie forest, Winnfield, and greater Dry Prong.

South of Alexandria, he could find Cajun music on the radio. He listened to "Valse de Kaplan" and "Mamou Hot Step." In the early afternoon, passing through Mamou, he slowed to look over the plain brick facade of Fred's Lounge, home of the Saturday morning Cajun music broadcast, chanky-chank dance, and peppermint schnapps binge. A few Mamouans stared at him and his cruiser.

Bubba Fusilier Chevrolet looked pretty much like car dealerships everywhere since the 1970s: white metal building, generic plastic signage, big American flag. When Maytubby parked on the new-car lot, no salesman rushed out the door to greet him—maybe a first. When he pushed into the frigid showroom, no one stirred from their cubicles behind the floor. As he passed the cells, each occupant was typing furiously away on a computer. He walked toward Service, past bathrooms and a water fountain. In a little office, a young woman looked up at him. The nameplate on her desk said she was Bennie Schexnaidre. She saw him looking at it. "Bennette," she said. "Can I help you?"

"Nice to meet you. My name is Bill. I'm looking for the sales manager."

"What kind of cop are you?"

"Tribal police. Chickasaw Nation, in Oklahoma." He showed her his badge.

"Never heard of Chickasaw. We got Houmas. What you doin' down here, *shah*?" She made a puzzled smile.

"Working on a case with the Oklahoma Bureau of Investigation. We want to find someone we think bought a car here."

"I better help you. The sales staff is overwhelmed." She smiled at her monitor. "As you could see. Have a seat."

Maytubby handed Bennie Schexnaidre copies of David Woodley's Oklahoma driver's license and his registration for the 2004 white Cobalt coupe. Before she accessed the database, she stared at the photo.

"Do you recognize this man?"

"Hmm."

"By another name, maybe?"

She shook her head and began typing. Maytubby heard one of the salesmen creak up out of his chair and walk across the showroom. A door beeped to announce it was being opened. The thick, pleasant nasal timbre of Cajun speech bounced among the shiny cars.

"That matches our records." She picked up a pen and wrote on the registration copy. "This is the local address he gave us. It's in Mermentau, just a few miles south of here on Ninety." She pushed the papers across the desk.

"Do you mind if I show this photo around?"

"Let me. Here." She took the enlarged copy of Woodley's license, rose from her desk, and led him back to the showroom.

The walk-in and the salesman who met him stopped talking, and the other salesmen looked up. "Any you know thiz guy? He bought a car here couple years bag." She held up the sheet, and they came quickly, eager to identify the crook—even the customer, who seemed to forget his mission. They stared at the redheaded man with asymmetrical eyes.

"Nat boy'z uu-*glee*," said the walk-in.

"Yah," the other said, nodding. Then they shook their heads.

The service manager, walking outside the showroom glass, saw the gathering and came inside to see what the excitement was about. He didn't recognize the redheaded man, but he said, "I can tell you dad's not *the* David Woodley. You know whad ..." He grabbed a small phone book off a salesman's desk and flipped through it. "No Woodleys."

Bennie Schexnaidre said, "His address then was in Mermentau."

The service manager pointed at the photo and looked at Maytubby. "Tague dad down to Mermentau and show it aroun' at C'est Si Bon and Sonnier's. Somebody know dad levee rad."

Maytubby folded the photo and registration and touched his forehead. "Gentlemen, Ms. Schexnaidre. Thank you very much for your time." When he started the cruiser, he could see the group in the showroom staring at him.

Ten minutes later, still checking his mirrors, he was crossing a muddy Bayou Mermentau on US 90, which became Railroad Avenue in the little town on the east bank. A few blocks in, after passing a few defunct storefronts, he found Sonnier's Grocery. It was a freestanding clapboard building with a broad, flat facade like those in Westerns. A flat metal canopy with rod supports ran the length of the beige building.

Maytubby's arrival brought the manager out of his cubby. A few shoppers craned to appraise him. Studying Woodley's photograph with an impatient frown, the short, middle-aged manager, who wore an unconvincing honey-blond toupee and a red tie striped with RAGIN' CAJUNS in black, squinted and wrinkled his nose but did not shake his head too forcefully.

"He looks kind of familiar, but I can't put a name on him."

The manager took the photo from Maytubby and showed it to the cashier and a stocker. They shook their heads in turn. Black ceiling fans wobbled and thumped, and the stocker hefted a bushel of okra down the produce aisle. Maytubby bought a package of Konriko brown-rice cakes, made just down the road in New Iberia, and two bananas from Costa Rica.

The last few pickup trucks of the lunch rush were parked under live oaks in front of C'est Si Bon, a faded gray flat-roofed restaurant near the south edge of town. Patrons were drifting out—mostly men, snugging their dozer caps, some lighting cigarettes. As Maytubby approached the door, a sweet gust of sautéed onion and green pepper and fried shrimp swept over him. His mouth watered, and he regretted the bananas.

A warhorse Ford 350 pulled into the lot and parked by the kitchen entrance. On the driver's door, someone had stenciled SHRIMP + FISH. Two bearded, sun-creased men in wifebeaters, jeans, and white rubber shrimp boots got out and began unloading ice chests. They did not look at Maytubby. After they had gone in the kitchen, he walked to the rear of the truck and waited. Eventually, they returned with an empty chest. When they saw he was holding papers, they scowled at the ground.

Maytubby introduced himself and explained his errand. He showed them the photograph. One of the men shook his head and walked away. The other stared at the photo and squinted. Then he flicked the paper with the nail of his middle finger. "Basile Trepanier. Egsept he had brown hair. Come from way up Bayou Neh*pee*kay."

Maytubby could spell the person's name but not the name of the bayou. He took out a pen and held it over the paper. "Nezpique," he wrote, as the man dictated. Tattooed nose.

"I wend to school wid dad guy. 'Mullet,' we called him. 'Cause of his eyes."

"When was the last time you saw him?"

"High school. He lef' outta here long time ago."

"Can you tell me where he lived?"

"Won't do you no good. All his people long dead, place sold."

"Anything unusual about Trepanier? Besides his eyes."

"Oh, *shah*." The man smiled and shook his head. "Nothin *usual* aboud Mullet. Smart but"—he put an open palm in front of his chin and then flicked his hand away—"*coo-yon*. Crazy."

"He gay?"

A shrug.

*　*　*

Maytubby drove past the address on the Cobalt's bill of sale. There was a number on the house, but no roof.

The Jefferson Davis Parish Sheriff's Department was on Plaquemines Street in Jennings, in a tall, modern red-brick building shaded by live oaks that were already ancient when modern came along. A young deputy named Thibault examined Maytubby's badge. The sheriff was busy, and Maytubby could see that Thibault was hesitant to open his files to a tribal policeman. Shouldn't have used the word "nation." He took Scrooby's card out of his wallet and handed it to Thibault. "This is my boss at OSBI. Give him a call." Maytubby smiled. "He might grouse at you, but he'll identify me."

Thibault frowned less and waved the card away. He typed Trepanier's name into the computer and found people with that surname, but no Basile. "Our computerized records don't go back a long way. We're gettin' there." He disappeared down a hallway and returned a few minutes later with a thin file. He opened it for Maytubby to hold like a book.

The face in all three mug shots of Basile Trepanier was a much younger, auburn-haired version of David Woodley, but they were the same person. The meager beard and shoulder-length hair on the younger man didn't change the face much. Trepanier's eyes, despite the territory between them, held a kind of furtive insolence.

The file documented three state charges over the course of four years: forgery, deceptive trade practices, and illegal gambling. In the second case, he was accused of taking large deposits from northern Louisiana residents for an alligator hunt that never materialized. Trepanier had been acquitted of all three charges.

"Deputy Thibault, do you know anyone who might remember these trials?" Maytubby handed him back the file.

Thibault stuck his thumbs in his duty belt and drummed on it with his index fingers for a few seconds. Then he pointed at Maytubby. "Miss Bernadette. She'll be smoking on her bench."

Thibault introduced Maytubby to Miss Bernadette, a stout woman in her seventies who was indeed smoking on her bench, and told her what the tribal policeman wanted to know. He showed her the mug shots. She clamped a Marlboro Gold long between her lips, took the file with both hands, and held it as close to her face as the cigarette would allow. A dirt bike blatted down Main, and Maytubby looked at it over his shoulder. Blue.

Miss Bernadette closed the file abruptly, handed it back to Thibault, and shooed him away. She patted the bench for Maytubby to sit beside her. But after he sat, she didn't face him. Instead, she spoke as if she had an audience: turning her face from side to side and gesticulating. In an incongruously soft voice, she said, "Dawlin', I don't know where that lawyer came from and I don't know where he went back to, but he was one hell of a lawyer. He got that Trepanier boy off every time. Lord only knows how he got paid or *if* he got paid. That batch of Trepaniers was poor as dirt.

"After Basile ..." She bent her head toward Maytubby, still not looking at him, whispered *"Fou"* out of the corner of her mouth, and then resumed her story aloud. "After he suckered those old boys from Shreveport believing they was going on a gator hunt, the prosecutor thought he had him over a barrel. Those boys paid Basile three hundred dollars each. In advance, in cash, which they sent through the mail. When they got to the end of the road down here, where he told them to meet him, he showed 'em a little johnboat 'bout as big as a shoebox. Not even a motor, just *paddles*." She chortled. "He gave 'em a map he had made in pencil that told them where to find the gators. The prosecutor held up that map in court. It looked like one of the gators drew it. You couldn't tell where anything was.

"But by the time that jury was charged, Basile's lawyer had made those poor men from Shreveport look like city slickers who expected to be treated like English lords on safari in Africa. 'Maybe these gentlemen have brought charges against my client because he didn't put them on a yacht and stock the galley with champagne!' Oh, but he was good."

"Do you remember his name?" Maytubby said. "If you don't, I can look it up."

Miss Bernadette held her cigarette at arm's length and studied it. "A funny name. He didn't talk like anyone around here. A Bible name first and an ugly name after."

"Goliath Butts."

"No, not Goliath Butts." After a beat, a little wheezy chuckle rose from Miss Bernadette. "You," she said. She took a deep drag on her cigarette and then tossed it under a boxwood bush.

A mockingbird ran the gamut of its impressions, from cardinal to chuck-will's-widow, to squalling baby. Distant thunder from a sea-breeze squall on the coast echoed off the red-brick wall. "You made a joke," she said, "but you were close. Scab, stob, cob ..."

Maytubby had not seen this coming. "Solomon Stoddard?" he said, unable to keep the rush out of his voice.

Now Miss Bernadette did look at him. "How did you know that?"

"I didn't."

CHAPTER 21

Maytubby rarely ate sausage, but the scent rolling out of the smoker at Cormier's Specialty Meats made him dizzy. As he walked under the store's sign, which bore a large red cayenne pepper, he reminded himself of his charge: buy tasso for Hannah Bond. Ten minutes later, he emerged with a small ice chest stuffed with tasso, boudin, andouille, and chaurice. He told himself he had many friends.

While his cell was ringing Jill Milton's, he scanned the parking lot and the street. No dirt bikes, no black sedans. Jill was still at her nation office. Maytubby told her about the shooting and assured her that the gunman had absconded into the darkest Ouachita and not pursued him. He told her the sheriff was keeping a close watch on Love. She was quiet. "You remember the preacher in the Cobalt—the guy with Johnny Rotten hair said he was a preacher?"

"Satan is Waitin'?"

"The same. He's from a little town down here. Name's Basile Trepanier."

"Bastille—as in French Revolution?"

"No 'T,' one 'L.' Petty crook after he dropped out of high school. Charged with three felonies. Never convicted. Had a hot-wire lawyer who appeared from thin air whenever he went astray. You'll never guess who."

"Perry Mason."

"Solomon Stoddard."

"No."

"Improbable."

"Impossible. What in the name of Pete was he doing down there? Not defending the downtrodden."

"You don't think he was burnishing his humanitarian creds?"

"Pfffft."

"You're likely right."

"He probably had ulterior motives—an intricate strategy for preserving the Oklahoma way of life. Whatever that is."

"Don't pretend you don't know. You're just playing dumb while you go about destroying it."

"*Shhhh.* Don't tell."

"Want to have breakfast at the Aldridge tomorrow morning?"

"If you promise to wear your policeman hat."

* * *

Six hours later, in Paris, Texas, Maytubby watched an orange sunset, filtered through steam rising from a Campbell's soup plant. The scene had a postapocalyptic feel.

He didn't have a grand unified theory yet—just some general suspicions. Stoddard was cultivating Trepanier, a poor young sociopath who needed help and money. Maybe sex was involved, maybe not. Jennings, Louisiana, was physically and culturally a long way from Oklahoma City, and even early in his political career, Stoddard could not have afforded to be seen defending a hoodlum. In Jennings, he might as well have been recruiting in Albania. Had he recruited others? Was he after a mischief maker? A hit man? A go-between? Muscle seemed unlikely. Trepanier looked mean enough, but on the small side for a head cracker.

In the dark, Maytubby wound down the little bluffs of the Red

River and returned to Oklahoma. The name was Choctaw, a language very close to Chickasaw, and meant "red humans"—that is, Indians. How strange to see a sign that read "Welcome to Indians."

Before midnight, he was standing in the foyer of the Pontotoc County Jail, stretching his back and blinking in the harsh light. There was a little trail of blood on the floor, and the air smelled of booze and sweat.

The dispatcher's name was Judy. Her eyes were red, and she yawned and stretched. Maytubby asked her if someone had told Love about the shooter on the motorcycle.

"Yeah. They said he didn't say nothin'."

"Shocking."

Crickets chirped down the hall. Someone deep in the jail yelled something unintelligible.

Maytubby bade Judy a good night and walked out into the hot night. Though the jail was surrounded by buildings—civic offices, banks—their parking lots were empty. Downtown was dead as the Martian plain.

Love was not his responsibility now. And the unsavory fellow was behind some stout walls. There was likely a deputy back among the cells. Maytubby had not slept, to speak of, the night before. And he had driven twelve hundred miles.

A half hour later, he was parked across Townsend Avenue from the jail, between two city cars, e-mailing updates to Scrooby and Bond. He typed fast so he could douse the blue screen light. Nobody had shot up his house—or torched it. Still, he had twisted all the mini-blinds shut before he stowed the Cajun meats, brewed coffee, and iced it in an old thermos jug.

A bat juked around a street light, feasting on insects. Far to the south, a BNSF engine blew for a country crossing. Maytubby fought sleep by imagining the train's progress from quarry to quarry, up into town. He heard the crossing bells on Mississippi, and the horn fading in the direction of Kansas City.

Had the early morning not been so still, the noise wouldn't have awakened him. A distant tenor whine, its pitch rising and falling. His wristwatch said 4:20. The bat was gone, and there wasn't a car on the streets. The cycle was coming off the State 3 bypass. It wasn't a dirt bike. Something weightier, but not a cruiser or a touring bike. It was coming fast, not stopping for lights or signs.

Maytubby sat up and shook his head. He was thirsty and took a pull of iced coffee. He called the jail and told Judy not to buzz anybody in. Then he hung up before she finished her first question. The cycle shot past Townsend, made a U-turn on Main, made the wide left, and roared toward the jail.

Reflected streetlamps raced like tracers over the rider's black helmet. His sprinter's crouch on the sport bike all but obscured his visor. He wore black gloves. Abruptly, the whine fell silent, and the bike, a green Ninja ZX-11 with the "Kawasaki" taped out, veered toward the jail. Maytubby waited until the rider dismounted before starting the cruiser and juicing it across the street. The rider spun on his feet and faced the headlight glare. He was holding a gray blob of something. Two holsters hung at his sides, bulging with what looked like bottles.

Maytubby flung open the door of his cruiser, but before he could draw his pistol or shout a command, the rider had emptied both holsters and launched their contents in two directions: one over the jail wall and one toward Maytubby. From his crouch behind the cruiser door, Maytubby followed the arc of the object. In the reflected glow of his headlights, it looked like a beer bottle in a paper sack. He leaned on his right haunch and deflected the thing with the heel of his left boot. It made a shallow arc and smashed on the asphalt, sprouting tentacles of flame. Behind the wall, the jail facade danced in the glow of a second fire.

The rider was on his unlit bike and fifty yards down Townsend before Maytubby could follow, riding always being faster than driving. Maytubby radioed the Lighthorse dispatcher and could briefly see her through a window at headquarters as he sped past. She said she would call the fire department and alert the sheriff and the state cops. By the time the bike moved out of the acceleration lane onto State 3, it was doing well over a hundred. The cruiser's big hemi was straining as Maytubby tried to see anything useful before he ran out of streetlight—and before the bike outran him. There was no tag on the bike, and though the tail lamp was unlit, he saw that the red lens was chipped.

On the deserted four-lane, Maytubby pushed the cruiser past 140. A nighthawk sailed out of the brush beside the road and burst like a feather bomb on the grille. The Ninja screamed as it pulled away from him. A Pontotoc Sheriff's cruiser with a full head of steam joined the bypass at 377, its strobes lit. The Ninja slalomed around it and plunged into darkness. As Maytubby slowed, he saw the Ninja's lights flick on just as the Pontotoc cruiser's strobes flicked off.

Maytubby followed the cruiser to a crossover and parked beside it. When their windows came down, he saw the smiling hatchet face of Katz. "Phoo-*ooo*!" Katz said. "You need a jet engine strapped on your car to folla that thang."

"Yeah."

"Get up early to get some coffee." Katz smiled and shook his head. "Teach me. Ever emergency vehicle in the town is rollin', the jail's on fire, and I get a backup call on a pursuit. Order a coffee and end up in the got-dang end times."

"That guy on the bike was trying to kill Love."

Katz gaped. "You mean burn him up like that guy in Antlers?"

"Wiley Bates."

"You think it was the same guy."

"I don't know. Or the same guy who shot at me last night." Maytubby put his finger in the exit hole.

"I heard about that, too. You're onto some badasses."

"Or one badass who gets around."

"What kind of bike was that?"

"New green Ninja. I think—the make was taped out. No tag. Rider was wearing a black helmet and gloves. Some sort of backpacking holsters attached to a belt. I think they call it a hydration belt. Stowed his fire bottles in there. Used reactive paper instead of wicks. Bike had a chipped taillight."

"I'll call it in to OHP Troop E and Coal and Johnston."

"Thanks for that, Katz."

"No problemo."

Pools of water on Townsend Street reflected the strobes of every emergency vehicle in Ada. One fog machine short of a rock show, Maytubby thought. He parked outside the crush and walked to the rear of the jail, where he found a rank of prisoners shackled in a chain gang. They wore navy-blue jumpsuits. A young deputy stood in front of them, cradling a pump 12-gauge and yawning loudly. He nodded at Maytubby in midyawn. The air smelled moldy and acrid.

Love was the last prisoner in the rank. The deputy understood, detached him from the others, and chained him to a stanchion. Maytubby stood near Love but did not look him in the eye. He looked away toward the gray light in the east. "He went after me before he went after you. But he got Wiley. You know that?"

Love stared into the strobes.

"Wiley's a lump of charcoal in Antlers."

Love showed nothing. He had been in Mac a good spell.

The young deputy walked toward them. "Better talk to Sergeant Maytubby, Love. He saved your bacon this morning."

Maytubby and Love both ignored him, and he walked away.

"Guy who tried to shoot me—and probably the guy who killed Majesty Tate—dressed all in sand camo but not real camo, rode a dirt bike same color. Don't know if the same guy did this." Maytubby tilted his head toward the jail. "He was dressed in black, helmet same. I chased him. He was riding a big Ninja, so I didn't chase him for long. Same wiry build as the other biker. You got a name?"

Love's face wore the vacancy of death.

The east grew rosier. One by one, the strobes went dark and the vehicles rolled away. The young deputy conducted his charges back into the jail. The fire had burned two juniper trees and licked at the eaves of the jail before the trucks arrived.

As Maytubby walked toward his car, the Pontotoc County sheriff, Carl Driscoll, hailed him, motioning toward the jail entrance. Driscoll wore rumpled street clothes, and his thick white hair geysered above his sleep-creased forehead. He pointed to a dollop of plastic explosive on the street, its fused blasting cap sprouting from the top like a seedling. Crime tape snaked under a circle of rocks around it.

"DIY," Maytubby said.

"Easy as biscuits."

"Going to blow the door." "Looks that way."

"Don't think I'd want bottles full of gas on my pants when I lit that fuse."

"You'll always have my vote, Sheriff."

Shaking his head, Driscoll clucked and said, "That is a dangerous bastard."

CHAPTER 22

The Aldridge Coffee Shop, on Main Street, was bright and noisy. Fluorescent light pooled on the flatware and plates. The café smelled like fried bacon, with faint vestiges of tobacco smoke. The walls were hung with framed photos from the thirties and forties: Ada High football teams, men holding up bass and huge yellow catfish, a rank of Aldridge waitresses in white aprons and maids' caps. Once, the place had been part of a busy hotel. Then motels changed the hotel into an apartment building. Maytubby stole Wi-Fi from one of those apartments to send Agent Scrooby a lively account of the bomb thrower. To Hannah Bond, he e-mailed just the facts, in two sentences.

The Aldridge clientele may have been mature, but when Jill Milton strode in with the morning sun at her back, forks hung in the air and conversation ceased. She wore a black poplin sleeveless dress with a V-collar, black lace crochet tights, and black suede wedges. Tossing her black thatch as she pulled off her sunglasses, she spotted Maytubby at a table near the plate-glass window. She settled her purse and laptop and sat. Customers resumed eating and talking.

"You're not wear … Bill, what's wrong with your eyes? You smell like smoke."

"I just got out of the shower, too. But the other, yeah. Full night."

The waitress brought Jill coffee. Maytubby ordered oatmeal with raisins. Jill studied his face as if it were lacerated. She ordered Cheerios and a banana.

He smiled. "Are those stockings code?"

"In letter."

"But not in spirit."

"Not really. What happened last night?"

He told her. Their food came, but she didn't touch it. "He's a guerrilla," she said. "He rides back into the hills. He might have burned your house, too."

"I wasn't home."

"You should stay with me. How can you eat oatmeal when it's so hot outside?"

"Because I really want steak and eggs and biscuits and gravy, and if I'm going to be virtuous, I want to be rewarded with a little pain. Not a lot of pain."

"Where's your policeman hat? I did my part."

"It kind of got burned up. The physics were pretty complicated."

"You want to stay with me till you get this psycho?"

"So I can protect you?"

"I was thinking more because he probably doesn't know where I live and you'd be safer there. But yeah, sure, so you can protect me."

"Your Cheerios are getting soggy. Why the heels and tony hose?"

She appraised a spoonful of cold mush. "You're right." She ate it and frowned. "Going to Lawton to talk to the Comanche Nation about the Eagle Play. There's some interest in it."

"Better warn them about Solomon Stoddard."

"The scourge of Paoli? Were the state cops able to connect him to Satan is Waitin'? The Bastille guy …"

"Basile. Trepanier. I'll find out this morning. Meeting with

Scrooby in the city. I promised Hannah some tasso from Acadiana. She'll be in Connerville this afternoon. When I learn what she knows, I'll know what I have to learn."

"Dare I ask what tasso is?"

"Delicious, is what."

She nodded, frowning. "I thought so."

CHAPTER 23

As Maytubby crossed the higher ground between the Washita and the Canadian, he noticed that mature trees were dying—something he had never seen. Every livestock pond was dry, and there were very few cattle. He passed a flatbed semi hauling hay. Minnesota plates. He saw no suspicious motorcycles.

His cell rang as he was admiring the healthy cottonwoods on the banks of the South Canadian. He stopped on the apron of a defunct Sinclair station. It was Lynn Washington, the man from Hope. "Sergeant Maytubby ..."

Maytubby could hear it in his voice. "Boone is dead."

"Yes sir," Washington said. "I questioned him yesterday. Learned nothing. Last night, he was strangled with a bootlace next to his car when he got home from a bar. Neighbor in the mobile home park heard the scuffle."

"When?"

"Just before midnight."

"Motorcycle involved?"

"Everybody in the park heard it."

Maytubby told Washington about the arsonist's sortie.

"No flies on that mofo."

"Not a one."

At one time, Oklahoma City covered more square miles than any other city in the United States. From the most southerly additions of brick ranchos to OSBI headquarters in the northern part of town, Maytubby drove seventeen miles. The agency lived in a glass house, a cube resting on a squat plinth between a food warehouse and a freeway. A guard waved the Lighthorse cruiser through a substantial iron fence.

Scrooby was banging his fist on his forehead when Maytubby arrived at his office on the third floor. "Pissants!" he said, throwing his hands up and tossing back his head. "Agh!"

Maytubby waited for the squall to pass. The agent waved him in, reached for a folder on his desk, and clicked his laptop mouse. "Tate, Tate, Tate. Here we go."

"Where do you go for ribs?"

Scrooby looked up. "Huh?" He wrinkled his nose, ready to pounce on the non sequitur.

"Ribs. You were eating ribs when I called about the arson in Antlers. There was love in your voice."

"Oh. Leo's. To look at it, you'd think it was a bait shop. Until you get close enough and that hickory comes in your vents. Then Leo's got you in his power. You can't proceed."

Maytubby opened a small paper sack and pulled out a generous link of chaurice. "You like smoked sausage?"

"*Oh*, yeah." Scrooby took it and lifted it to his nose. He closed his eyes. "Sweet."

"It's the Cajun version of that Mexican chorizo."

Scrooby rolled sideways in his chair and stowed the sausage in a mini fridge. "Can't even grill it in my own backyard. Damn burn ban. Didn't stop that peckerwood last night, though, now, did it?"

"If you outlaw fire, only outlaws will have fire."

Scrooby blew a raspberry. "Tate ... Tate. Oh, yeah." He looked from the folder to the laptop screen. "In the Cobalt, we found some hair and got DNA off straws and other stuff. Love had been in that car. But nothing matched the DNA under Tate's nails."

"That was quick. Was any of the hair red?"

"No. Da-da-da, Woodley—your whatever-Frog-name …"

"Trepanier."

"Treepanty rented the run-down Dairy Whistle month-to-month for the Sun Ray Gospel Fellowship. Neighbors say he had a small crowd Sunday mornings for the last year or so, nothing the last couple of weeks. Nobody recognized Tate from the photo."

"Show the neighbors one of Stoddard?"

"Oh, right."

"You find a congregant?"

"A what?"

"Somebody who went to the Sun Ray church."

"I'm afraid they're gone with the wind."

"You get a warrant and search the building?"

"We looked in the windows. Big windows. Nothing in there but some trash."

"You find any other connections between Woodley-Trepanier and Stoddard?"

"No."

"You find out if Stoddard was ever seen around the Western Sky or Old Route Sixty-Six?"

"No."

"No, you didn't look into it?"

"Correct."

"But you will."

Scrooby looked at him. "Stoddard is a stock member of the Oklahoma City Country Club. In Nichols Hills." He jerked his thumb in the direction of the affluent neighborhood a short distance from where they were sitting.

"What's a stock member?"

"Invitation only. Small club. Exclusive."

"Any idea why Majesty Tate would have the address and number of the pro shop there?"

"You said nobody there had ever seen her before."

"Probably out of the question to show her photo and Stoddard's together."

Scrooby said nothing.

"Oklahoma History Center?"

"Oh, yeah. Nobody working there yesterday recognized Tate."

"On my way here, I got a call from my Arkansas CID man. The first suspect in that CODIS-match murder was strangled last night by a man who left the scene on a motorcycle. The victim and Love were exculpated by the same DNA."

A siren whooped on the freeway. The scent of burnt coffee drifted into the office.

"*That's* why you were at the Pontotoc jail last night. Law's not taking the bait."

"Right. Amino acids trump cunning. He's got to clean up the old-fashioned way." "Today the proud owners of green Ninjas all over Oklahoma want a piece of that jackass."

"And Woodley-Trepanier is the only person we know to look for," Maytubby said. "Anybody else can just ride away."

"Gotta start somewhere. Can't swab everybody. Can record the names and check 'em in the database. One of our detectives is calling all the cycle dealers in the region to see who bought both a green Ninja and a camo Suzuki RM-Z250."

"You think our guy's that stupid?"

"Maybe he didn't see needing both at once." Scrooby said. "We're checking the either option, too, Bill. And yes, I know, he probably stole it or bought it used." He gave his mini fridge the side-eye.

Maytubby understood that in a few minutes he would be competing with his own bribe. So he stood and took a step toward the door. "What do *you* think Stoddard was doing, down there in Cajun country defending a local crook who reappeared as a preacher with a different name in his old district?"

Scrooby smiled archly. "Giving him a leg up?"

CHAPTER 24

The khaki smoke of a wildfire smudged the horizon ahead of Maytubby as he passed Sully Wolf's dogtrot and mounted the old Wanette bridge over the Canadian. The camelback trusses threw jittering shadows across the cruiser's dash. A Chinook bearing water to the fire beat the air not far above the rusted iron. At Byars, he detoured west and suddenly found himself in a refugee caravan. Horses and cattle in trailers, dogs standing atop household goods hastily piled in the beds of pickups.

An occasional gust carried smoke across the highway. The fire was close and coming fast. Livestock driven out pasture gates—cattle and horses, even some goats and sheep—emerged ghostlike from the smoke on dusty section roads, trotting blindly onto the highway. A whitetail doe hurdled a compact car in front of him. Refugees gave the animals' panicked rush a wide berth. Maytubby turned on his strobes to show drivers behind him where the road was.

His radio popped. "Hey, Bill."

"Sheila."

"How close are you to Ada?"

"West of Byars. In the smoke."

He heard Sheila talking to someone else. She came back.

"McClain sheriff wants you to evacuate the roads between One Seventy-Seven and Three West. He says go fast, be rough, and take as many as can't drive in the cruiser. This thing is blowing up. Red Cross is setting up in Konawa."

"Sheila, could you radio Hannah Bond and tell her what I'm doing?"

"Yessir. Oh, and Fox wants—"

"Will evacuate. Out."

As Maytubby neared the first major intersection, the line of traffic sped up, and he gained a little head start on the fire. Inbound brush trucks from volunteer fire departments north of the Canadian howled toward him. Not many people lived on the dusty section roads, but some of the houses had long driveways. Both his siren and his strobes were on, and he fishtailed on every turn. As he approached the houses, mongrels bit his fenders, and chickens fled. In most, he found no one at home, but he rousted a few citizens who were shocked to look out their front doors and see a wall of smoke looming over the russet prairie.

By the time he reached the apex of his assigned triangle, the first houses where he had stopped had already flared. A peeling cottage surrounded by potted flowers was the last house before his highways joined and crossed the Canadian. There was no car in the drive. He pounded on the screen, rousing a small black dog that yapped and scratched furiously at the aluminum frame. Somewhere in the house, a woman was singing.

> There is pow'r, pow'r, wonder-working pow'r
> In the blood, in the blood, of the lamb, of the
> lamb ...

She sang off-key. She was stout and elderly, slicing okra in deadly heat, without electricity. When he laid a hand on her shoulder, she flinched and lost her balance. He caught her and turned her to face him. Her grimace revealed gray dentures. A wave of sour breath made him turn his head a little. "A wildfire is coming. Fast. You have to evacuate."

She watched his lips and his eyes. "Talk louder."

He took paper and pen from his pocket and wrote in big letters: FIRE. LEAVE NOW.

"I don't have no car." The dog set his front paws and barked shrilly.

He motioned for her to follow and bring her dog. Her eyes got large and red, and she turned round and round. Then she threw up her hands, shook her head, and began to untie her apron. Chasing the collarless dog around Maytubby, she finally lassoed it with the apron's neckstrap and fashioned a makeshift collar and leash.

Maytubby shook a sofa pillow out of its case and began snatching photos from tables and walls and sliding them into the case. The woman grabbed a tattered patent leather purse. She motioned the officer to a deep drawer, where he found two old leatherette photo albums, which he jammed into the pillowcase. Also, a rusted baking-soda tin, which he knew held her cash. He threw that in. She watched him, nodding and weeping. The dog had clearly never felt a collar or a leash. It snapped at the apron and whirled like a dervish.

The old woman pulled the dog with all her might. Slimy okra caps stuck to her forearms. Maytubby took the apron leash and dragged the writhing dog to the cruiser, where he gently boosted it with the toe of his boot into the trunk. It was hot there, but the dog could make it the six minutes to Konawa. He tossed the case into the backseat, settled the woman on the passenger side, her sweaty knee against the stock of his shotgun. She had not visited a bathtub in a good while.

They were over the Canadian in two minutes, soon speeding due east, away from the fire's path. The woman waved her hands over her head and rocked forward and back with her eyes shut tight. "Sweet Savior, don't let the fire burn my house. I don't have no insurance, Jesus." In the trunk, the black dog barked frantically, its tone different from earlier. "Lord, oh my Lord, spare my house!"

A few of the same pickups Maytubby had seen fleeing the fire were parked in front of Konawa High School. Red-faced men, women, and children stood beneath the awning of a Red Cross van from Shawnee, drinking cold bottled water. Maytubby parked under some shade, wrapped a rag around his hand so the dog couldn't bite him, and managed to get the creature tied to a water faucet standpipe. He turned on the faucet and let the dog lap.

He helped the woman into the cool foyer, where the Red Cross was already setting up cots. He eased her down onto one, laid the pillow case and her purse beside her, and brought her some water. "I'm Bill Maytubby," he shouted. "What's your name?"

"Odelia Johnson. Folks call me Deely. You think that fire'll get my house?"

"I hope not." He offered her his cell. "Anybody you need to call, let them know where you are?"

She looked at the phone, then at him. "I never used one of them thangs. Can you call my brother in Tecumseh?" She knew the number.

Her brother told Maytubby he would pick up his sister and her dog as soon as he could navigate around the fire. Maytubby relayed this to Odelia Johnson and gave her his card. "I'm usually in Ada. Call me if you need anything."

"I 'preciate it. Now, I don't have no phone, son." She slid the card into her bosom. One of the Red Cross volunteers offered to look after the dog, and Maytubby was on his way to Connerville. As he crossed the Canadian again, a dozen miles east of the fire, field pumpers from Ada met him coming the other way. A dazzling white pyrocumulus blossomed above the smoke—the only cloud in the hot sky.

Ten miles down the road, the smoke and fire were barely visible. Trees were exploding, thousands of acres burning, houses and barns being vaporized, families set adrift. A little more than half an hour had passed since everything in the path of the fire was as it had been for a long time, give or take a few births and deaths. In another half hour, Maytubby reckoned, the fire and its refugees would begin leaving his emotional territory, and in a day they would be receding in his memory. The automobile, television—strange how modern humans sampled disaster, coming and going, passing through.

Where US 377 transected the boulder field, the spot where Hannah Bond had broken Majesty Tate's lugs free, Maytubby saw the deputy's cruiser parked behind another car. Bond was standing at the other driver's window, handing him a citation. She stood with her back to Maytubby, so he pulled onto the shoulder and waited until the speeder had pulled away.

In front of the Tin Can Café in Connerville, Maytubby was only half out of his cruiser when Bond said, "Where's my tasso at?"

"I was going to surprise you."

"How? By bringing me something I asked for?"

"Good point." He pulled the keys from his pocket, then froze. "Ah, crap."

"You forget my surprise?"

He unlocked the trunk and raised the lid slowly, peeking in.

Hannah Bond laughed. "What's wrong, still on the trotter?"

He opened the trunk lid all the way, and they stared at shredded Styrofoam spattered with cayenne sauce. In the fire commotion, he hadn't even noticed the carnage.

"All right, Sergeant, you surprised me after all." She shook her head. "One of them swamp bears get my tasso?"

He slammed the trunk. "Evacuated a woman to the Red Cross in Konawa …"

"Hungry, was she?" Bond raised an eyebrow.

Maytubby snorted. "That lady was so hungry, she was cooking *okra.*"

"Well, in that case, I don't mind losing my tasso. I hope the Red Cross trims her nails."

An RC Cola thermometer nailed to the doorjamb registered 112. They sat at a gray Formica table. Hannah Bond ordered a chipped-beef barbecue sandwich with fries. Maytubby ordered sides of boiled carrots and beets. Bond said, "Seriously?" and looked up for sympathy from the waitress, who smiled and gave her the side-eye.

When the waitress had left, he said, "Benny Magaw going to bust in on us and tell you to get to work?"

"It's my lunch hour. Besides, yesterday, which I spent in the city, was a day off." She pulled a small spiral pad out of her pocket and flipped it open.

"You wear your uniform up there?"

"They'd think I was a rent-a-cop. Or 'What's a deputy from Bumfuck doing asking me questions?' I wear a white shirt, my duty belt, with my badge on the belt. You can't see the writing on a badge."

"Scrooby won't touch Stoddard."

"Old Sol's a law-and-order man, Bill." Hannah made a crooked smile.

"Didn't seem that way in Louisiana."

From her notebook she pulled tightly folded photocopies of Stoddard's old state senate campaign flyer and Majesty Tate's driver's license photo as it was reprinted in the paper. "Waited till the caddies at OCCC started leaving. There weren't many. I managed to show the photos to two. Both recognized Stoddard, but the second one ..." She looked at her notebook. "Josh Perkins. Said he saw Tate parked in front of the club a few months ago. He never saw them together. He also said she looked different someway. And she wasn't in the Aveo."

"Please tell me it wasn't a Cobalt."

"Not a Cobalt. It was a beater, an old Corolla." She licked her thumb and flipped the page of her notebook. "Now. I wondered how Majesty Tate could look different someway but still enough like herself for the ID. Unless she wore sunglasses, her eyes would get your attention. Lips next, especially for a kid like Perkins."

"So you're talking giant red *Pretty Woman* Vivian wig."

"I thought she would pick the other one—the peroxide pixie one. So, with my trusty Swiss Army Traveler scissors, I made her one from a scrap of newspaper. Then I waited until it was almost dark and went back to your motels, the Western Sky and the Old Route Sixty-Six. Could be we got different shift clerks. Anyway. Nobody had seen Stoddard at either motel. Of course, he wouldn't like to show his face at a mom-and-pop motel in the city where he lived. When I held the little white wig over Majesty Tate's hair, both clerks recognized her."

The waitress brought their orders. Maytubby, smelling the oak-smoked meat and the splash of bourbon in the sauce, bent to his microwaved vegetables with a great unfulfilled longing.

"Too much to ask for a Lexus, I suppose."

"Too much to ask for the motel guys to remember a Lexus. They remembered that nothing about the car stuck out, so no, probably not a Lexus. No security cameras, which you know. She rented rooms several times, under different names and car makes and models, always paid with a fifty. Neither guy could remember or find any of the names she had used. But 'Majesty' nor 'Tate' rang a bell. They both said they didn't alert the owner or the cops, because she had good manners and didn't wear too hooker-y clothes."

"'Not too hooker-y.'"

"I don't want to use their words." Bond frowned and looked down.

They ate without talking. Short-haul bobtails and propane trucks rumbled by on the highway. Whenever a motorcycle buzzed past, both of them looked it over.

Hannah Bond mopped up the last puddle of sauce with a shred of white bun and pushed her clean platter away. "Fox going to let you keep working on this?"

"Probably not. Can I have your newspaper wig for my Tate picture?"

"Yep. You going back to headquarters now?"

"No, back to the city. By way of Denver."

Bond looked out the window. "We're going to bring the sons a bitches down, aren't we, Bill?"

"You betchum, Sam Ketcham."

She continued to watch the road. "My daddy used to say that."

CHAPTER 25

The dome of the state capitol, rising behind the tattered facade of the Sun Ray Fellowship, glowed orange in a cloudless sunset. Maytubby parked the cruiser down the alley and walked, scanning the commercial strip for motorcycles. He also listened. Sun-melted tar in the lot stuck to his shoes as he tried the rear door. It was locked. The dead bolt, he could see, had not been thrown, and the knob lock set was new and cheap. He kicked the knob off.

The last appliance had long ago been dragged from the former Dairy Whistle's kitchen, leaving a confusion of capped pipes and hoses and vents. The place gave off a smell of rancid lard, bringing up memories of his great-grandmother's kitchen. The cinder-block building was an oven. The huge tempera sunrise painted on the plate glass jaundiced the light inside. One broken metal folding chair on the concrete floor was all the furniture left from the mission. Even the pulpit—which every mission had to have—was gone.

Maytubby played his flashlight along the baseboards. Dead roaches, chewed pens, an ant-picked mouse skeleton in a sprung trap. And wedged behind an electrical conduit, an order of service photocopied on canary paper. Maytubby saw that Pastor Woodley had awarded himself a doctor of divinity degree. His sermon three weeks ago was titled "God Is My Fuel Injector." On the program, a child had drawn stick figures shooting stick guns at one another. The bullets were dashes. Above them some m-birds, and above those a sun. Next to the reverend doctor's name, the child had drawn a frowny face with its tongue hanging out.

The previous week's attendance had been thirty-two, the collection seven hundred twelve dollars and thirty-two cents—not too shabby for a bush-league fraud.

Maytubby searched through the participants to find those with unusual names. Jim Brown, the music leader, was out, as was Jaime Gómez, the guitarist. Elaine Arnholtz, the keyboardist—now, she was in. Maytubby folded the paper. He inhaled deeply but found nothing new in the air—still the trace of rancid grease. His great-grandmother had kept a rusty can of fresh lard next to her stove. Scooped the fat out with a spoon and then, with her index finger, launched the little white sailboat out onto a hot iron skillet, where it skated round and round till it sank into its own sea. Everything from okra to fry bread to pork chops, catfish, chicken, and dredged bacon went into that lard sea. And emerged sweet and brown and crisp.

Walking out the back door, he saw the breadcrumb stuck to paving tar: Satan is Waitin'. The tar was a nice touch. But the brimstone tract had no connection with a Sun Ray Gospel Fellowship, which clearly looked on the bright side. The songs on the order of service were "God Fulfills Me" and "My Soul Soars." The good reverend doctor's sermon comparing the Creator to an auto part was neither Jonathan Edwards nor Joel Osteen. Trepanier was just bin-picking props. He had probably heard enough words in some little Acadian Catholic church to fool people who might have been reared in church but not in any denomination—people who didn't know felix culpa from SpongeBob SquarePants.

Elaine Arnholtz lived in half a brick duplex near Oklahoma City University. She was in her midtwenties, and when she first spoke, her voice told Maytubby that she was a nonsmoker from somewhere in southern Arkansas. She was fair and plump, with long blond hair and a pleasant, open face. After he identified himself and asked if she could answer some questions about her pastor, she didn't grow defensive as he had expected.

"Okay," she said. "Is Dr. Dave all right? He just vanished into thin air a couple of weeks ago. He doesn't answer his cell. Has he done something wrong?"

"I don't know where he is, either. I wish I did. As far as I know, he hasn't done anything wrong."

"Is he an Indian? He didn't look like an Indian."

Maytubby smiled. "I don't know. How did you find out about Sun Ray?"

She tugged at her earlobe. "Oh! I saw a flier in Coffee Slingers. I'd been looking for someplace where I could worship without following a lot of rules and getting guilt-tripped into a slew of responsibilities."

"What sort of a pastor was Dr. Dave?"

"Real energetic. Made you feel good when the service was over. Folksy, I guess. He told funny stories."

"What kind of stories?"

"Oh, about people in the country."

"In the bayou country?"

"Yes, he did, and he had that cra-a-azy accent. It was so cute."

"He ever talk about damnation?"

She lowered her face and shook her hair. "Oh, no. I would never go to a church like that. It would put me in such a bad mood, I could never commune with God's spirit."

"Do you know where your pastor earned his degree?"

Elaine Arnholtz looked at the ground. Looking up, she made a little moue. "You know, our fellowship wasn't into rank and degrees and status. He never used any fifty-cent words."

"Why do you think he would use the title and print it before his name?"

"I guess if I went to all the time and effort to get a doctorate,

I'd sure put it in front of my name." A little snap of defiance there.

"Did you notice what he drove?"

"Yeah, but only because it's the same as mine except the year and color. He drove a white Chevy Cobalt."

"He never drove anything else?"

She shook her head.

Maytubby showed her photos of Solomon Stoddard and Majesty Tate. Stoddard's photo was not on a campaign flier. She didn't recognize Tate. "I've seen that guy a lot on television. He's a politician or something. I mute him."

"Why?"

"He's a gasbag. Plus, there's something creepy about the way he always talks about family values but then struts around with his tarted-up whichever-number wife and never has raised a child."

"Lot of that going around."

"Doesn't make it any easier to swallow."

"Did you ever see this guy, Solomon Stoddard, with Dr. Dave?"

"You gotta be kidding. Dr. Dave wouldn't go within a hundred miles of a fraud like that."

"Is Dr. Dave married?"

"He's a widower. His wife was killed three years ago by an amoeba she contracted when she was swimming in the Washita River."

"How awful."

"Isn't it?"

"Do you know where he lived?"

She frowned, tugged her earlobe again. "Over in the eastern part of the state. He had another congregation over there. That place. He made jokes about it. Tushie?"

"Tushka. Except nobody has lived in the Tushka house listed on his driver's license for years, and his real name isn't Dave Woodley."

Elaine Arnholtz narrowed her eyes and said nothing.

Maytubby handed her his card. She looked at it a couple of seconds before she took it.

"I'm sure it's not true."

"Thank you so much for your time. If you see Dr. Dave, I would appreciate it if you would get in touch with me."

She shoved the door with a very cold shoulder. The door didn't make it all the way to the jamb, which spoiled her exit. As he walked away, Maytubby waited for the door to slam, but it never did.

CHAPTER 26

Solomon Stoddard lived in a large brick Georgian Revival house off Hudson Avenue in Heritage Hills, a neighborhood built by oil in the first decades of the twentieth century. Many of the old houses had fallen into disrepair before the neighborhood gentrified. The houses were well drawn and built to last, so that in the twilight Maytubby couldn't always tell which ones were decrepit survivors and which were *re*vivers. Water rationing had eliminated one clue: the sun scorched the lawns of rich and poor alike. On his first pass by the house, he couldn't be sure, but it wasn't likely that Stoddard's stone-fox wife would live in a dump.

Though surveillance in a marked cruiser was never a good idea, Maytubby didn't have much time, and it was, after all, the age of the rent-a-cop. The black Lighthorse cruiser would incite curiosity while there was still enough light for people to read the lettering, but in the dark it would simply be welcome security—to most residents. So, with an hour of dusk to kill, Maytubby drove over to Super Cao Nguyen, in the Asian District. He walked under glowing plastic palms and into the busy market, where he bought a vegetarian bánh mì sandwich, a carrot, a mango, and a cup of iced sugarcane juice. Eating the sandwich in his cruiser, he listened to a *Radiolab* show about the foot-long mantis shrimp, which has eyes with three times as many photoreceptor types as humans, trinocular vision, and mighty claws. Mantis shrimp were known to have stowed away in pieces of coral that ended up in aquariums, where they emerged, killed and ate every other living thing in the tank, and then smashed the glass.

Streetlights flickered on up and down Classen Boulevard, and the last sunlight backlit a few fair-weather cumuli. Maytubby wondered what ultraviolet light looked like to mantis shrimp. He drove to Automobile Alley and bought a large cold-press at Coffee Slingers, then called Jill Milton and told her he wouldn't be needing her protection tonight. He reassured her that he had not been tailed by any motorcycles. Then, when it was good and dark, he went into Heritage Hills and parked away from streetlights, next to a huge oleander on the cross street nearest Stoddard's house.

Very few cars passed. An upstairs light was on in Stoddard's house, but drapery covered all the windows. Over the next few hours, lights went on and off, upstairs and down. Crickets were rubbing up a respectable din. Exactly at midnight, the house went dark.

With spare napkins from Super Cao, Maytubby blotted sweat from his face and neck. It was still in the nineties, and the air didn't stir. He hated surveillance, even on mild days. His coffee was running low, and he was sleepy. At half past two, a 1970 Porsche 914, its targa popped, squealed around the corner behind the cruiser and turned in two doors down from Stoddard. Two young men, drunk and talking loud, got out and peed into the shrubbery. One of them shouted, "*Nev*er, *nev*er!" Then they went inside. Maytubby ate the carrot. An hour later, he ate the mango.

At half past five, he was awakened by newspapers slapping driveways. It was an hour before sunrise. A light was on downstairs in Stoddard's house, toward the back, near the garage. A few minutes later, one of the two garage doors shuddered up, its guide wheels shrieking, and the bulb in the opener housing revealed an empty bay. Maytubby could see the side of the Lexus next door. So the wife wasn't home. He pulled his short-barrel binoculars from under the seat.

Headlights approached fast. The car that wheeled into the light of Stoddard's garage was a white 2004 Cobalt coupe. Maytubby nodded in the dark. Last car the law would be looking for. The garage door closed before the driver got out, so Maytubby trained his glasses on the short walk between the house's back door and the side door of the garage. The back porch was not lit, and the only light on inside the house went out. He put the glasses down.

The house looked dark, but the downstairs windows had a dull glow from a lit interior room. The air was still very warm. AC condensers buzzed on and fell silent up and down the street. A mockingbird set up a twelve-tone ruction. A BNSF freight blew for crossings in Deep Deuce.

The garage door shuddered and shrieked open. If Stoddard was going to conduct clandestine all-hours meetings in his house, he needed to invest in some WD-40. Maytubby watched the Cobalt drive away from him and make a left. Instead of following the car, he drove parallel to it. The Cobalt made the first left and drove right in front of Maytubby on Nineteenth Street. He waited for it to go over a little rise before tailing it. There weren't many cars on the road, which was both good and bad. He wouldn't lose the Cobalt, but he couldn't easily hide the hulking Charger. He hung back several blocks, stopped when the Cobalt stopped at Classen Boulevard. It went left on Blackwelder and turned into the drive of a simplified prairie duplex from the thirties. A dead elm loomed in the front yard.

Maytubby kicked the cruiser so he could stop Trepanier before he got inside. The yellow light from a sodium street lamp turned Dr. Dave's hair a sickly orange. After memorizing the Cobalt's tag, Maytubby lowered his passenger window and shouted, "Trepanier!"

The man spun around and dropped his keys on the porch steps. Maytubby got out of the cruiser and walked quickly toward him. There were no motorcycles in the yard, no garage at the end of the drive. The sky had brightened enough to show the bafflement on Trepanier's face as he squatted to retrieve the keys. He had waited too long to dye his hair, and his brown roots were visible. Maytubby introduced himself.

"How can I help you, Officer? What were you saying to me from your car?"

"Your name. Basile Trepanier."

"My name is Dr. David Woodley."

"The one from Tushka who lives in a house that's been unoccupied for years?"

"That's an old address. When I moved to the city, I forgot my new address when I wend to the DMV the next time."

"You told the good people at Sun Ray that you lived in Tushka."

"I still have a little prayer meeting congregation there Wednesday nights. And I lige my privacy. I'm more lige an evangelist than a traditional pastor."

"How do you come to call yourself a doctor?"

Trepanier tilted his head back a little. "I have a doctor of religious research in scatology from Christian Soldiers Seminary."

"A Christian seminary in the United States offers a degree in excremental studies?"

Trepanier shook his head and smiled with pitying condescension. "No, Officer. Scatology—the end times as foretold in scripture."

"That would be *es*chatology. Are you pre-, post-, or amillennial?"

"Pre," Trepanier said neutrally.

Maytubby said nothing for a few seconds. He wanted Trepanier to sweat his bluff. "What were you discussing with Sol Stoddard at his house just now?"

"He asked me to pray with him before he began his busy day."

"Solomon Stoddard belongs to Frontier Baptist Church. He's a bigwig there. That church has three assistant pastors. None of those men could minister to Mr. Stoddard?"

"He asked for me, and I came."

"Did he ask you to pray with him at Boggy Depot State Park?" Trepanier stared at him.

"And you know, what I can't figure out is why Solomon Stoddard would go all the way to Jennings, Louisiana, *three times*, to defend you in court."

"You're *coo* … razy."

"I know he has something on you—nothing that would ever really get in your way. I also know you have something on him— something that would ruin him."

Trepanier began to laugh. "You barkin' up the wrong tree."

"What tree is that, Basile?"

Trapanier shook his head in wonder. "That is the stupidest name I ever heard. The Lord have mercy on a man called that."

"And double down on a boy called 'Mullet.'"

For an instant, the insouciance drained out of Trepanier's face. He tossed his keys in the air and caught them. The condescending smile snapped back in place. "I think your police work has got you mess up. I can answer your questions, Officer, but it won't profit you." He was juggling idioms and breaking some dishes.

"Maybe you're right," Maytubby said. He didn't want to go too far before Scrooby could be convinced to question him. "Thank you for your time."

He walked to the cruiser and heard Trepanier unlocking the door to his apartment. Before Maytubby reached the street, he heard a dead bolt hit its strike. Then another. Then another. Dr. Dave had been to the hardware store.

And he wasn't afraid of the Lighthorse Police. The neighborhood didn't look menacing. He wasn't the type to subscribe to a newspaper, but there was a TV dish on his roof, or he could mooch enough wireless to learn about the fires in Ada and Antlers, and the Ouachita shooter—if he hadn't done those things himself. Basile Trepanier was looking more and more like a flight risk. Scrooby wouldn't be in his office for another hour.

Maytubby swung by the two motels again to see if he could

turn up a clerk whom neither he nor Bond had interviewed. He immediately recognized the sagging green polo shirt of the Western Sky innkeeper, so he drove on to the Old Route 66. There he found a very young man, maybe eighteen, with a geyser of gelled black hair and a zirconium nose stud. He wore black nerd glasses and a faded brick-red T-shirt and was sorting a pile of room keys on numbered plastic paddles, left by departing guests.

"Hi," the young man said. "Help you?"

Maytubby smiled and laid the photos of Stoddard and Tate beside the room keys. The young man cradled his chin on a palm. He tapped Stoddard's picture. "I've seen him, wearing some weird hat and sunglasses, coming out of a room a few times. Always number fourteen or fifteen—the ones farthest from the street, back by the hedge. He must have got the room from the person on the night shift. I come on at six. He stared at Tate's photo and bit his lip. "Nnnnn." Maytubby slid the newspaper wig into place. The clerk's eyebrows went up. "*Oh*, yeah," he said, nodding. "She and this guy came out of the room at different times, but they got in the same car."

"Which was …?"

"White compact. Chevy, maybe. Plain, like a rent-a-car."

"You mind Googling '2004 Chevy Cobalt'?" Maytubby bent his head toward the massive old cathode monitor on the desk.

"Sure, but it might be Tuesday before it comes up."

He was right.

A motorcycle roared by on the highway. Maytubby looked out the window and listened until the sound went away. The shadow that the motel's saguaro sign threw on the street looked like a shot from a fifties sci-fi film: the shadow of the alien raising its stiff arms with clumsy menace.

"That's it," the clerk said. He couldn't find any record of the car or the license number Maytubby gave him.

"When did they start coming here?"

"I don't know. I just started here mid-May, when classes ended.

I saw them a few times this summer, not often. Not for the last couple of weeks." He didn't ask why Maytubby was asking. Either incurious or discreet. Maytubby was betting on discreet.

"What's your name?"

"Gill Bowers."

Maytubby handed Bowers one of his cards. "Call me or e-mail me if you see or remember anything else."

"Will."

The Cobalt was still in Trepanier's drive when Maytubby detoured through the Plaza District on his way to OSBI. He wished he could summon an officer to watch the place, tail Trepanier if he left.

Early rush-hour traffic clotted I-44. At the I-235 interchange, excavators and dozers ripped out swaths of prairie blackjack oaks that had miraculously survived development on every side. The machines cut huge gashes in the red Permian soil for a nest of overpasses. The carcass of a young whitetail buck was splayed on the shoulder.

At OSBI headquarters, Maytubby sat in a folding chair outside Scrooby's office until he padded in just before eight. "Shew-ee, it's hot out there!" He unlocked his door, then turned to face Maytubby. "Ugh." He shook his head. "I can't deal with this on what my wife made me eat for breakfast. You know what it cost me to get those ribs I was telling you about?" His hand chopped the air. "What did I have for breakfast? *Oat*meal. With *skim milk*." He unplugged his laptop and cradled it under his arm as he pointed out the door and shut it behind him. "Lord above, you can't get your work done without real breakfast."

When they had settled into a booth at Classen Grill, Scrooby waved away a menu. "I know what I want." Maytubby scanned his quickly and ordered Memphis French toast and fresh-squeezed orange juice. Scrooby ordered biscuit debris, cheese grits, and sausage. He drank coffee and looked around the dining room. "Place is not much to look at, but they put real food on the table."

"And chickens on the wall," Maytubby said, looking at the gallery of rooster prints.

Scrooby said nothing as he drummed his fingers on the table and watched a tattooed waitress refilling coffee mugs. Maytubby drained his several times because he badly needed sleep and Scrooby wouldn't talk until he got food.

When the plates came, Maytubby pushed his fried toast to the side and made short work of the bananas and peanut butter. Scrooby perspired as he trenched into the biscuits.

"Now," he said, pushing his shiny plate away and belching politely into his napkin. "What are you doing up here again? Doesn't your nation need you?" He pulled a Swiss Army knife out of his pants pocket, winkled the plastic toothpick from its nook, and put it to work.

"Those things have *toothpicks*?"

"You think the Swiss Army lives on vegetables ..." He looked at Maytubby's plate. "Like you?"

"Stoddard ..."

Scrooby threw up his hands, rolled his eyes. "*Here* we go. Like I said, isn't your nation calling?"

"Hannah Bond ..."

"*Han*nah? Now we've got Johnston County deputies on the case? You do realize, Bill, that my agency was created to assist people like you and Hannah, who have limited resources."

"Hannah Bond's sister was raped and killed by her foster father. The Tate murder was committed in her county."

Scrooby frowned and looked out the window.

"Hannah stuck a blond wig on Majesty Tate's photo and found a caddy at OCCC who said he'd seen Tate sitting in a car in the club lot."

"Ever with Stoddard? No."

"No."

Scrooby turned up his palms.

"Hannah showed the wig photo to the same motel clerks who

didn't recognize her earlier. This time, they did."

"Silver wig sucks up a lot of attention." Scrooby thumbed his chin. "Don't see the face under it so well. You might put a blond wig on Winston Churchill and they'd ID her.

"One clerk we hadn't talked to, the morning clerk at the Old Route Sixty-Six Motel, told me this morning that he saw Stoddard and Tate getting in the same car—a white 2004 Cobalt—several times over the summer. Not in the last two weeks, though. Tate always checked in, used aliases and fake tag numbers. Paid in fifties."

"You think this was Treepanty's car before half its backseat went up in flames?"

"I don't know. I do know Trepanier drove a white oh-four Cobalt to Solomon Stoddard's house at five thirty this morning and stayed half an hour. I followed him to his apartment on Blackwelder. He said Stoddard had asked him to pray with him before the start of his busy day." Pious man that he is.

Maytubby drank more coffee. Scrooby sighed and dragged his laptop across the table. He said nothing as it booted up. When he had finished typing, he looked up at Maytubby. "Where was the hottie wife while all this was going on?"

"Stoddard has a two-car garage. Only his Lexus in there until Trepanier showed up."

Scrooby typed some more. He stopped suddenly and said, "Maybe you should e-mail all this to me."

"And here I was feeling so grateful for your assistance and resources."

Scrooby growled and shut the laptop.

"Inside the Dairy Whistle / Sun Ray Gospel Fellowship, I found an order of service."

"You get a warrant?"

"Place vacant, door ajar. Almost an attractive nuisance."

"Why, I'm surprised at you, Sergeant." Scrooby raised one eyebrow.

"I doubt that. One of the congregants listed on the order of service expressed great affection for 'Dr. Dave,' as the mission folks called him. He was folksy and had a wild accent. She asked if I knew what had happened to him. She couldn't tell me where he got his doctorate or what it was in. Trepanier told me it was from an institution called Christian Soldiers Seminary."

"Online for-profit, right?"

"On its website, credit card logos appear before the holy cross does. Accredited by God alone and, apparently, proud of it."

"Why would he still live so close to his church people? Seems risky." A tattooed male server stiff-armed the kitchen door, and the smell of sage and frying meat drifted into the room.

"I don't know. He and Stoddard obviously need each other. And religious charlatans can always say, 'God told me to leave this place and go to another place.' God tells them to do anything they want to do."

"You think he's the Ninja guy?"

"Don't know. So far, I haven't seen that trapdoor in his eyes. Or any bikes around his apartment, which doesn't have a garage. No tracks, either—and most of the grass burned off that lawn years ago. When I left Trepanier's apartment, I heard him throwing a bunch of dead bolts."

"You think he's scared?"

"Maybe."

"Who do you think Treepanty might be afraid of?" Scrooby said.

"If he's not the Ninja guy, then him, for one. If he is the Ninja guy, he's got enemies who won't wear funny hats and ask him nice."

"If he hasn't killed them all."

"He hasn't killed Austin Love. Whether Trepanier is the Ninja guy or not, he should be afraid of Austin Love."

"How much longer can Pontotoc hold him on the parole violation?"

Maytubby scrunched his face.

"I'll see if I can get a plain car over there."

Maytubby gave him Trepanier's address and license plate.

"That's right, you can remember stuff."

Maytubby shrugged.

Scrooby's cell played a perky digital mix of "Final Count-down." He looked at the screen, then took the call. Maytubby downed his orange juice. Scrooby said, "Really ... Huh ... Yeah ... Thanks." He put the phone in his pants pocket and said to Maytubby, "Wiley Bates, the Antlers charcoal briquette, bought a green Ninja three months ago. Davidson Kawasaki, in your nation's capital." Scrooby laid a twenty on the table, tucked his laptop under his arm, and stood up.

"Somebody we already didn't have to worry about."

Scrooby looked down at him. He shook his head, turned, and blew loud enough to make the passing waitress glance over at them.

CHAPTER 27

The deer carcass on the shoulder of I-44 was being scraped into a fill slide by a construction company front-end loader. The image rose up of the grisly buzzard in the crooked house, and Maytubby drove on past his exit. Instead of leaving the city, he went back to the Plaza District. The Cobalt was gone, as he knew it would be. He parked two blocks from Blackwelder so he could be a generic cop when he showed Tate's photo to Trepanier's neighbors.

Maytubby scanned the block for houses that might belong to older retirees—Buick in the drive, (dead) tomato vines in the side yard, rain gauge on the fence, geraniums in pots, venetian blinds. The first door he knocked on even had a crocheted curtain behind its three little windows. A fresh-faced woman in her late twenties opened it. She held a blond toddler with brimming brown eyes. Maytubby was happy to be wrong. She would see better.

He led with the wig. The woman swiveled her torso to calm her child. She said no to both the wigged and the nonwigged versions of Tate. "But I'm only here a few hours a day. I'll get the lady who owns the house." She walked toward the back of the house, the child staring soberly over her shoulder at Maytubby. Photographs of birds and flowers hung on all the walls, and some vases painted with more birds and flowers stood on the faux mantelpiece. The corduroy couch was festooned with doilies. He wanted to lie down on that couch and sleep around the clock.

A very tall woman of about seventy walked into the room with long, slow strides like a wading bird. She covered the distance to Maytubby in three steps. Then she stood still, hands clasped, and peered down at him. Her eyes, behind half glasses, were kind and inquisitive, and she smiled faintly. He lifted toward her face the blonde version of Tate and asked if she had seen this young woman in the neighborhood. The woman tilted her head back to look through the half glasses. Farsighted was good.

Maytubby took the wig away. The woman's expression didn't change much when she said, "Yes, Officer." She beckoned him to follow her and took two steps to the picture window facing Blackwelder. He took four. On a sewing table near the sill, he noticed a pair of old, durable binoculars. Maybe military, maybe German. They looked heavy, but it was clear this person could manage them. Beside the glasses lay a worn copy of *Birds of Oklahoma Field Guide*. Its spine was duct-taped. This was better than the half glasses. Maytubby suddenly felt less sleepy.

The woman opened the blinds about two inches and looked over the top of her glasses. "The birds don't notice you so easily." She turned to Maytubby. "And neither do the people." She smiled, pointed to the window, and leaned forward. In the back of the house, the toddler laughed sharply. Maytubby stood on his toes to see what the woman was pointing to. Trepanier's house with no car in the drive. "She was in and out of that house in the late spring and early summer. I haven't seen her in several weeks. I can't sleep anymore, you see. She often came home early in the morning, driving that little white car—or another one just like it. The guy who seems to own the car would take it and be gone for a long time, maybe a week. Sometimes, she took a cab; sometimes, another car picked her up."

Maytubby pulled out his phone and found a photo of a white

Lexus ES of the correct year. He showed it to the woman.

"Maybe. I'm not sure."

"The guy?"

She shrugged. "Never spoke to me or anybody. Landlord mows his grass—when the grass is alive. I think the guy dyes his hair. And his eyes are wide apart. Like a little child's, but wider even. Sundays when he's here, he goes out with a Bible."

"Ever see anybody except the girl over there?"

"Once in a while, a car at night. Couldn't see the car, just the lights."

"No motorcycles?"

"Don't recall any."

Maytubby stood very still. "You've been most helpful, ma'am."

"It's not out of the goodness of my heart. That little son of a bitch sits on his front porch and shoots songbirds with a pellet gun."

Maytubby handed her his card and wrote down her name and telephone number. "The State Police may contact you soon. I'm assisting them. They have limited resources."

"Has that man done something nasty?"

"We don't know. We're gathering information."

"And the girl?"

"She was murdered in Pontotoc County several days ago."

"*Ugh.* Wild beasts roaming the land, and you can't tell one from the milkman."

Maytubby nodded for the two seconds it took his synapses to patch the call to "milkman." "Yes, ma'am. Thanks again."

Coming down the steps, he saw the OSBI plain wrapper parking a block down Blackwelder. He turned away from it. In his cruiser, he e-mailed Scrooby the latter half of their conversation in the Classen Grill, along with what he had learned from the birdwatcher. And that Trepanier had left before the unmarked car arrived. He rolled down his windows and listened. No cycles in the immediate vicinity.

On the road back to Ada, Maytubby stopped in downtown

Norman and got coffee at the Gray Owl. Vintage bicycles hung from the ceiling, and small expressionist acrylics were mounted on the painted brick walls. The coffee of the day, noted in pink chalk on a blackboard, was La Golondrina—the swallow, as in bird. Okay pun. Pastries glowed in the vitrine. He added a date bar to his coffee and paid. Ceiling fans moved the cool air. The young faces bent over laptops were half lit by retro lamps. A few people were bent over Bibles; he could tell by the leather-grain binding. There was a token hipster presence—some tattoos and funny hats.

Maytubby looked from face to face, taking in the smooth skin and bright scanning eyes. The large, live room was quiet save for "Rocky Raccoon" playing softly in the rafters, and the occasional hiss of a steam wand.

In the Canadian bottom, fields of desiccated soybeans and corn rolled past his window like a russet carpet. Here and there an alfalfa patch, irrigated by a well, blazed green as Oz. Maytubby drank his coffee too quickly. To avoid seeing the fire damage, he drove farther south than he had to. He knew that the blaze had been stopped in the Canadian floodplain, which meant it was too small to trigger disaster relief. Lots of uninsured citizens in there. A Ninja passed him going the opposite direction. It was white.

"Agent Maytubby!" He flinched and realized he was on the edge of sleep.

"Yeah, Les."

"Your nation needs you."

"You been talking to Scrooby?"

"Doesn't mean he's wrong. I almost called you on your cell."

"Then you know that I had a productive stakeout."

"It's the state's case now, Bill. Let them and Johnston County handle it. I've got a subpoena needs to go to Tish yesterday."

"I'm about twenty miles out." Maytubby had the next two days off, but he did not remind his boss of this fact.

He stopped at a convenience store in Stratford and bought a large coffee. The woman who had kicked Donnie Frederick to the curb was in the checkout line. She gave him the stink-eye. He could try to thank her for her tip about the primered pickup, but she would just assume he was lying again. He pretended not to recognize her.

CHAPTER 28

Jill Milton stepped into her apartment, pulled her keys from the doorknob, and swore under her breath. "You scared the dickens out of me, Bill! Where's your cruiser?"

Maytubby propped himself up on his elbow. He had fallen asleep on her couch. "I parked it in back to outwit the guerrilla."

"I thought a male stripper had broken into my apartment."

"Comanches go for the veggie parable?"

"That was yesterday."

"I was just thinking those were some spirit-of-the-law panty hose."

"Nude. I had to do nutrition PSAs for KCNP this afternoon."

"Why does 'nude' sound like not the right thing to wear to do that?"

"I think the rule's logic is that if you don't wear panty hose, your legs are naked."

She reached under her skirt and snapped the hose off, balancing effortlessly on one leg and then the other to peel them off her feet. She made a nylon potato and threw it over the couch, into the front closet.

"Put it that way, I see what you mean. Woo-woo." He rose and walked toward her.

She put her hand out to stop him. "I have to shower. Spent most of the morning unloading produce and stacking zucchini and oranges in the FDP grocery store. Loading dock was hot as a skillet."

"You unloaded a produce truck while wearing a suit and panty hose?"

"Think about it. The alternative would be what, chinos and panty hose?"

"Okay, so back one more. Why were you working in the distribution store?"

"I was finished training a teacher in the demo kitchen, and a stocker called in sick. Not sick—bitten by a copperhead. Judy Cole."

He shook his head to show he didn't know her. "Where?"

Jill looked at him and smiled. "You are a man. So 'in the blackberry patch by her house on Kullihoma Road.'"

"That's sexist. I wanted to know where on her body."

"Huh."

"Huh. So where on her body?"

"Pinky toe."

"Did you wear one of those black support belts?"

"You have to shower, too." She dropped the venetian blinds on the west-facing window.

"You'll wash off all my pheromones and then yew won't wawnt me."

"You've been listening to country on that stakeout."

"So how is she? The stocker." Maytubby folded his uniform shirt and laid it over his duty belt on the coffee table.

"She's better. Told the manager her foot looks like a sack of dog food."

He turned the COLD knob in the little acrylic shower. "You want any hot in this?"

"No."

She grabbed a floral shower cap off a nail and pulled it over her hair. He fondled it with both hands. "Mmm-m. Victoria's Secret?"

She slapped his bum and shoved him under the nozzle. He pulled her in against him, and they kissed in the cool rain. French soap was one of Jill's indulgences. They lathered each other with Roger & Gallet Carnation. When the little round soap puck slipped out of her hand, Maytubby had to step out of the shower so he could bend enough to retrieve it. While he was stooped, she put her foot on his shoulder. He snatched it and bit her ankle.

She somehow managed to turn the water off before, soapy and wet, they tumbled out onto Jill's Guatemalan runner. She pinched the cap off her hair, and they made love under the faint chill settling from her window unit.

It was dark when they woke. A pale yellow light from the streetlamp on King's Road backlit the blinds. "This wool is scratchy," Jill said.

"'Hardwood' means what it says."

Maytubby had a shelf in Jill's closet where he kept a change of clothes, a toothbrush, a razor, and a paperback novel. The novel in there now was Stegner's *Angle of Repose*. He put on fresh jeans and a black twill short-sleeved shirt with a button-down collar. Jill pulled an almond knit blouse over her head and tugged up some olive Capris.

"Sustenance," she said. She opened the refrigerator and handed Maytubby a pear, a bag of arugula, a little package of walnuts, and a bottle of creole mustard. Then she hefted a large Pyrex casserole out onto the counter and opened the lid to show him marinated tofu strips.

"Looks like you've been to DK Nutrition. Olive oil, balsamic vinegar, and?"

"Soy sauce. You know the salad, right? Pears not too thin?"

"If they are, you going to curse and thrash me like last time?"

"Worse."

Long before Jill moved into the garage apartment, the pilot on the tiny old three-burner stove had died. A green spoon holder on the back of the range held a small stack of used Blue Diamond matches. She struck a fresh one and lit a burner, then blew out the match in Maytubby's direction.

"Devil woman!"

He halved the Bosc pear, cut a slice, and held it up to her.

"It'll do," she said.

He slid some walnuts into the toaster oven and whisked together olive oil, white wine vinegar, creole mustard, and salt. Jill slid the tofu slabs into a large skillet and leaned against Maytubby while he beat the dressing. "I don't know why people want big kitchens," she said.

When the tofu had crusted, she flipped it, spun her laptop on the kitchen table, and clicked on Pandora's Smooth Jazz. Maytubby set out plates and cutlery and poured ice water in red plastic tumblers. With one of the wooden matches, he lit a fat red candle. While Jill was serving the tofu, he drizzled the greens and pear slices with his dressing and topped the salad with walnuts.

He set the bowl on the table and looked over everything. "Where's the ketchup?"

"Sit down."

They clunked tumblers, and for a good while the only sounds in the room were the rattle of forks and the throaty moan of Chet Baker's trumpet.

"Trepanier and Stoddard *are* in cahoots," Maytubby said.

"You caught them cahooting?"

"Five a.m. yesterday, Dr. Dave Woodley paid a visit to the scourge of Paoli."

"*Dr.* Dave?"

"Christian Soldiers Seminary."

"Motto 'Onward!'"

"Doctorate in scatology."

Jill honked and turned red. "You're shitting me."

"Told me so himself."

"If he's in cahoots with Stoddard, he's got the right degree for it."

"Said Stoddard had asked him over to begin the day with prayer."

"What did the trophy wife think of … Wait. She wasn't home." Maytubby touched his nose.

"Do you think they're hooking up?"

"Not so much anymore, though it's not out of the question. I found a motel clerk who saw Stoddard and Majesty Tate together more than once. And a neighbor across the street from Dr. Dave said Majesty Tate stayed at his apartment in the late spring and early summer. Said he was gone a week at a time."

"The OSBI agent …"

"Scrooby."

"You convince him?"

"He didn't like it."

"Why doesn't he bring the Bastille guy in?"

Maytubby smoothed his hair. "He put a tail on him. But Trepanier took off after I talked to him. Before the unmarked car arrived."

"He's like a free radical, floating around somewhere, causing mischief."

"It may have caught up with him. He's got too many dead bolts on his front door. I also learned from an Arkansas State Police officer that whoever killed Majesty Tate killed a Realtor involved in a business dispute. The killer evidently set up a fall guy."

"Like Austin Love."

"Yes. And the fall guy was later strangled by someone on a motorcycle."

"The killer isn't a very good tactician."

Maytubby stabbed walnuts with his fork. "Forensics is thwarting a whole generation of cunning rogues."

"You still don't have DNA for the strangler or the person who tried to kill you, so …"

"Yeah, we could have two or three different people, and one of them could be Trepanier."

"Or Stoddard," she snorted. "Can you picture him on a dirt bike?"

"Not willingly."

"You need your Mountie hat when you talk like that."

"I'm secure in my imperialist identity."

Jill frowned at her salad. "I have this bad feeling you're going to drive around all night looking for trouble."

"I wouldn't know where to start."

"Does that mean we can read to each other and then spoon?"

"I think so."

He washed the dishes, and she dried them and put them in the tiny cupboard. "How long has it been since we did *True Grit*?" she said.

"At least six months. Took me a month of that to stop talking like Mattie Ross."

"Keep your seat, Trash."

"Exactly."

Jill took a well-handled copy of the novel from a shelf by her sofa and sat with her back against one arm. She put on her round black nerd readers, which she used when she had taken out her contacts. By custom, Maytubby faced her with his back against the other arm. They played a little footsie. She cleared her throat loudly and inhaled to begin reading.

Before she could, they both heard the climbing whine of a motorcycle. She laid the book in her lap, and they both looked at the floor, concentrating on the sound. It wound down South Broadway toward and then past them, on to Kerr Lab Road, fading out to the southwest.

The voice Jill Milton had invented for Mattie Ross their first time through the book was schoolmarm imperious. Maytubby laughed as she cocked her head back and delivered Mattie's backstory. Tom Chaney, the man who murdered Mattie Ross' father, "rode his gray horse that was better suited to pulling a middlebuster than carrying a rider. He had no handgun but he carried his rifle slung across his back on a piece of cotton plow line. There is trash for you."

Two hours later, Mattie was chasing Tom Chaney through Indian Territory and Jill was still reading. Maytubby was happy she hadn't handed the book back to him. She liked Mattie.

Just after ten, she closed the book and tossed it to the center of the couch. He wanted her to read the whole story and felt a little cheated by bedtime. She went into the bedroom. Maytubby checked his e-mail and phone messages, then plugged in both devices to charge. When he turned off the living room lamp, the charging and status lights of their devices on the kitchen table pulsed in a comforting way. They seemed to reassure him that everyone would stay close to him and that the simulacrum world of cyberspace would awake at his touch tomorrow and shelter him and his from life. If everyone kept their head buried in that world, the buzzards gyring high in the real sky would remain invisible.

Jill lay on her side on top of the sheets, the red T-shirt nightgown sliding off her shoulder. Maytubby carried his pistol into the bedroom and set it on the night table. As he was unbuttoning his shirt, Jill frowned at the gun. "It's the first time."

"Your house. Want me to put it back?"

"No. I know you don't want it there. You don't even like guns."

He took her in his arms and breathed the scent of her skin—cumin and green tea. He whispered in her ear, "Make sure I'm awake before I start shooting."

"Will do."

The window unit labored.

*   *   *

At 3:20 by the digital clock radio, Maytubby woke but lay still. Headlights swept the apartment ceiling, first one way, then another, switching directions too quickly for a car. So *a* headlight. The window unit almost masked a guttural thrum that finally registered.

He rolled out of bed slowly and walked to the blinds, lifted a slat. The bike was on King's Road, barely visible in the dark space between the illuminated cones of two streetlights. It was going in slow circles, round and round, like a Shriner's bike, but not a cruiser. Many of the houses on King's Road bore no numbers, Jill's garage apartment among them. The apartment was also set back from the big house—a hard place to find in daylight. The headlight went out, and the engine fell silent. A few seconds later, a narrow, intense flashlight beam from a few feet outside the big-house gate darted randomly across the lawn and the facade of the house. Jill's car wasn't in the garage. The flashlight beam paused on the rear of the old champagne Accord.

Maytubby didn't like that, though he couldn't immediately see what anyone but a cop could do with what was illuminated. He shucked on his civilian pants. Jill breathed thickly, her face to the wall. He took his pistol off the night table and grabbed his cell. Kneeling behind the couch, he opened the cell, dialed the Ada Police. The dispatcher, whose voice he didn't recognize, listened to his short backstory and his request for two cruisers, no lights or sirens, to block King's Road at Stockton and at Broadway.

He snapped the phone shut. As he was walking back to the window, he picked up Jill's reading glasses and slipped them on. He knew they had a low diopter and wouldn't blur the world. The ice-blue shard of light still played over the house, from the same spot. The person had not moved. Down in the bottom, a rooster crowed. He gave the cops almost enough time to arrive before he stuck the pistol in the back of his pants and stepped out onto the little wooden landing at the top of the stairs.

At first, the biker could not locate the sound of the long spring screeching on the old screen door. The ice-blue pencil zigzagged a few times before it found Maytubby, who, standing in his civvies, feet bare and nerd glasses in place, said in his best hick voice, "Hey, there! *You're* up with the chickens! What can I do you for?"

The blue light was intense, but Maytubby could see in his peripheral vision the prowlers arriving just seconds apart. The biker stood completely still and said nothing. Some coyotes yelped in the woods across the bypass. Maytubby pressed his palm against his jeans to keep it dry.

A minute or so passed. "Hel-*lo-o*?" Maytubby said. Nothing.

He couldn't tell exactly when the biker turned his eyes back to the street and saw one of the cruisers, but the flashlight went out, and the grate of heavy boots slewing on gravel brought Maytubby down the stairs. Even in big work boots, the biker was remarkably swift, and he had a twenty-yard head start toward the road. The Ada cops couldn't see them yet.

Closer to the road, there was enough street light to show Maytubby a green Ninja. Its rider leaped into the seat, and strobes from the Ada cruisers lit up the whole block. Maytubby couldn't shoot, because of the houses. He heard the full-throated scream of the bike's engine as he left his feet. Though the biker had not turned his helmet in Maytubby's direction, he instinctively flattened himself on the bike and even lowered his head below the gas tank, like an old pony trick rider. Missing the biker's torso, Maytubby caught a pinch of shirt as he tucked for the ground. He held on as some loose gravel on the asphalt ricocheted off his head.

The cruisers were getting closer, and the biker tried to drive with his right arm and drag Maytubby loose. He couldn't. He braked the bike, whipped off the T-shirt at shutter speed. Maytubby grabbed the tailpipe. It was not too hot, but it was slick. The Ninja shed him, roared into the bar ditch and around one of the cruisers, and screamed down Broadway. Both cruisers gave chase. He stood and watched them wind down to the bypass, slow, and turn off their strobes.

"This is tired," he said, and spat on his bloody elbow.

Jill was still sleeping when he got back into bed. The window unit had masked all the commotion. He tried to think of ways to catch the Ninja. All were magical. Soon he was asleep.

"You lied to me, Sergeant," Jill said as he walked into the

kitchen. She handed him a Frankoma cup shaped like an oil drill head and poured coffee into it. "You waited till I was asleep and then you drove around all night until you found trouble. You also bled on my sheets."

"I am a man of my word. Trouble came to me." He told her what had happened.

"So you blew our cover. The biker guy knows where we are."

"*Sí.*"

CHAPTER 29

Maytubby was emptying his mailbox of commercial flyers when his cell phone rang.

"Austin Love's bond has been set," Naomi Colbert said, "and his uncle is coming to pay it this morning."

"Surprising. The uncle, I mean. Love was stealing from him, and he knew it."

Colbert said nothing.

"Thanks, Naomi."

"You're welcome."

Maytubby opened his refrigerator and took out a few rotten crooknecks and tomatoes while pondering what Love would do first. He and Trepanier were the only bird dogs in Maytubby's kennel, and Trepanier was God knows where. He carried the vegetables out to the compost and then shot some scalding hose water on his pickup to wash off crisped pecan leaves and crow droppings. His old Ford, the nation's only unmarked vehicle, had a police radio but no air conditioner, and it was well over ninety-five already, the sun already up in the pecan boughs. Time's winged chariot.

He ran into the house and changed into his uniform. The

large bandage he had slapped on his elbow peeled off into his armpit. He put on his duty belt, balled up his civvies, grabbed an old straw farmer's hat, and sprinted for the truck. He inserted the absurdly tiny key and turned it, and the 352 V-8, big as a washing machine, its labyrinthine carburetor newly rebuilt, rumbled to life.

Hannah Bond answered her cell on the second ring. "Hannah, Love's coming out of Pontotoc this morning. You on shift?"

"No. But wait. You know OHP issued an APB for the Looziana preacher man in another damn white Cobalt? Well, your buddy Katz just lost him in pursuit in the boonies west of Boggy Depot. I don't know what Katz was doing down there."

Tumblers spun and clicked. Maytubby played out scenarios and then abandoned his plan to follow Love in the Ford. "You remember Love's pickup?"

"Yeah."

"What can you drive off duty?"

"Oh, Lord, my old Skylark."

"I'm going to get a plane and follow him in the air."

"The Lighthorse has an air force?"

"No, Heartland Aviation has a 1959 Cessna One-Fifty for rent. Could be a while before Love is out. Could be soon. I'll call you."

"Roger that. What's a Cessna One-Fifty?"

"Sort of like a photo booth with a wing across the top."

"Oh, yeah. We had one of them crash at the Tish Airpark. Had to use the Jaws of Life, except at that site it was the Jaws of Death."

"Thanks, Hannah."

"Anytime."

At a light on Mississippi, he speed-dialed the Heartland manager's cell.

"Hey, Frank."

"Hey. Is Two Niner Foxtrot free?"

"No. It's fifty bucks an hour wet, same as last time."

"Good one."

"Yeah, it's unoccupied. And topped off. Want me to pencil you in?"

"Starting now, for four hours."

At the Pontotoc jail, Maytubby nodded to Judy and was ushered into the cells. Austin Love was still there, sitting on his bunk, his gray eyes fixed on the wall. Maytubby said, "Mr. Love, Dave Woodley has abandoned his apartment in Oklahoma City." Love sat silent and did not move his eyes. As Maytubby was leaving the jail, he passed Carter Love, who nodded solemnly and bent to his familial duty.

Turning off Broadway into Ada Municipal, Maytubby glanced at the orange wind sock, which hung limp. He could use any runway. Inside the Heartland office, where it was cool, he phoned Sheila and asked her to call him when Love retrieved his pickup from Impound. He picked up the plane key at the desk. Rushing through the preflight, he shed his uniform shirt, duty belt, boots, and socks and threw them in the copilot's seat with a water bottle and field glasses. There was no AC in the 150, and he would be flying well below cooler air. "Clear!" he shouted out the side vent, though there wasn't a soul within fifty yards of the propeller. The little Continental engine caught instantly, and the prop wash blew a gale in through the vent. Maytubby put his face to the vent and kept his door open as he taxied. The barometer hadn't moved in days, so he didn't have to reset the altimeter to 1,016, the airport's elevation.

He scanned the taxiways and the sky. The airport serviced fewer than forty flights a day. He saw nothing. Still, he told the Unicom he was taxiing to runway 17. Before he entered the runway, he stood on his left brake and made the plane pivot in a circle so he could see every inch of sky. "Cessna One-Fifty Two Niner Foxtrot departing Ada on seventeen."

The runway was over a mile long—several jets lived in Ada—so Maytubby didn't have to use flaps. He shut his door, released the brakes, and pushed the throttle knob all the way in. The plane lifted off, and he gazed out the window to shift his brain into looking-down mode, seeing all the landmarks at once, unrolling like a map from horizon to horizon. It was much easier to misidentify roads and rivers when you flew above them.

He could see the four lanes of US 377 sprouting south. Jill had taken that road after he left her apartment. She was meeting with 4-H leaders in Milburn about after-school classes in Native American history and culture. After he leveled off at just three hundred feet, his cell played its jingle. Sheila told him that Austin Love had driven his pickup off the lot. Maytubby was already over West Main and saw the truck, its huge tires casting a big shadow, less than a football field's length below him, slewing around the cloverleaf and on its way south on the State 3 bypass. He called Hannah Bond and told her Love's direction.

Maytubby climbed to five hundred feet and stayed well behind the truck. Love was making over seventy—fast enough to be comfortable for the Cessna. The landscape was autumn brown, the ponds dry or just puddles crowded with livestock. At Ahloso, Love turned south on 377, shot around the little hilly curves at Fittstown, and made for Connerville. Maytubby called Hannah with an update. Then he called Scrooby's cell.

"Scrooby."

"It's Maytubby."

"Oh. OHP pissants lost Treepanty down there in Bumfuck."

"I know. Austin Love just bonded out of Pontotoc. Before he posted, I told him the preacher had left his apartment in the city. Love is tearing up Three Seventy-Seven, going south of Connerville now. I'm pursuing."

"What's all that racket? You driving a corn picker?"

"I'm in a plane."

The line went silent for a few seconds. "Wait. Whose plane? OHP's?"

"No."

"The Lighthorse has an airplane?"

"The nation has some planes, but not the kind that would help me. I rented it in Ada."

"Who's flying it?"

"I am."

Scrooby blew louder than the prop noise. "Wonders never cease. What the hell do you plan to do when Love gets to where he's going?"

"Tell you, for starters. So you can deploy your superior resources. Are you questioning Stoddard?"

"You hear me, Maytubby. You can chase Love to your heart's content. He's one of yours. But this murder investigation now belongs to the state."

Maytubby ended the call and watched Love's pickup leave the highway for a county road just west of the Blue. The pickup then headed south on what Maytubby recognized as Deadman Spring Road.

When he called Hannah Bond, she asked if she should leave Tish and head east toward Milburn. The town name caught him off guard. "Yeah, Hannah. In fact, Love is just now turning south on Forty-Eight-A. Jill's in Milburn today."

"Small nation."

A thermal jolted the Cessna and sent the cell into the copilot's seat. Maytubby fumbled for it and found it under his duty belt.

"You okay, Bill?"

"Bumpy today."

"Any guess where Love is headed?"

"No. Maybe he's jonesing and knows a stash. None of the gang I knew lived down here. He might have made friends in Mac. I'm hoping we can find out where he thinks the killer is—or whoever framed him, who may be someone else. It'll at least give us … Wait, I'm getting a call. Call you back."

"Bill Maytubby."

"This is Lorenza Mercante, in …"

"Coalgate, I know."

"What is that noise?"

"I'm flying."

"You mean like Superman?"

"Yes, ma'am."

"Listen, I read about Wiley. Spooky."

"Yeah."

"Anyway, this morning, when I was driving to the Brandin' Iron for breakfast, I saw a motorcycle in the driveway of Wiley's house."

"Could you describe it?"

"Kind of like a racing bike where the driver lays flat. It was green. No license plate. A guy wearing a helmet came out of Wiley's house with a little sack in his hand and drove away real fast south on Three. He was also packing. Legal now, if he has the paper. I went back to Wiley's house and saw the front door had been busted in. I called the cops."

"Thanks so much, Lorenza. Could you do me a favor and tell the Coalgate police to report this to Agent Scrooby at the OSBI?" He spelled the name. "You know OSBI?"

"Oh, yeah. What happened to Wolf Eyes?"

"He was innocent—of that charge. He just got out of the Pontotoc jail, and he's the guy I'm tailing."

"If you get tired of that, Coalgate's got an airport, too."

"I've heard that. Thanks again."

He called Hannah.

"Love is south of Milburn. Wait, turning east on …"

"Well, whichever one, it'll turn into Egypt Road. I'm catching up. I see your Spam can up there." The Cessna's vents, at three hundred feet, hosed him with hot air.

"This morning, someone spotted the Ninja shooter in Coalgate. Left south on Three."

"Maybe we should call in the National Guard."

"Who needs them? You know what they say: 'One riot, one Lighthorse.'"

"Nobody ever said that."

Maytubby throttled down to Love's ground speed. As Egypt Road stair-stepped along the margins of the Blue, he had to add flaps to fly slower still.

"I can see that goofy truck now. Shit-weasel just threw out a lit cigarette. We could do without another wildfire."

Between the Blue and Twelvemile Prairie were some square miles of wooded rocky land. From the air, one could see where driveways went, but on the ground they disappeared a hundred yards off the road. Love slowed and turned left, to the north. Hannah continued east toward the Blue. Maytubby saw a corrugated metal roof at the end of a long drive. A few hail dimples, a little rust, a stovepipe casting a crazy shadow. He could see no vehicles, but the area around the house was shaded. He banked away from the house and flew east. If Love hadn't picked him up already, he didn't want to push his luck by circling the house like a buzzard with a chain saw.

Hannah said, "That drive didn't have a mailbox, didn't have a cattle guard or a gate—or even much of a fence. Nobody's been running cattle in there for a long time, if ever. And it's three-point-seven miles east of State Seventy-Eight. After Egypt crosses the Blue, there's a farm trail goes back west and crosses the river at a low-water ford. I know the folks that own it. I'm going in, wade in the water."

"Be careful," Maytubby said into a dead phone. Seconds later, it came to life again.

"Maytubby."

"It's Jake. What's that racket?" Renaldo's phone was on speaker.

"I'm in a plane."

"Well, good for you. Sheila said it was your day off."

"I'm flying it. Love just bailed out of Pontotoc, and I followed him to a place east of Milburn."

"Wait. Shit." The phone clattered and snapped. Renaldo's siren whooped. There was a long pause. "I'm pursuing your Ninja with a cracked lens. Katz is behind me. He told me that bike was fast."

"Where?"

"Sixty-nine south out of Caney. Caddo cops are on the highway, but this guy will jump into the boonies before then."

"Your choppers are in Norman?"

"No, but they're both deployed far away. There he goes!"

Maytubby removed the flaps and throttled up. "I'm coming your way. What crossroad? Which direction?"

"Uh … Mount Carmel. West. It's dirt."

"Good. Slow him down, make him visible. Pillar of cloud by day. Matter of fact, I can see it from here."

With no headwind, Maytubby covered the distance in four minutes. The Ninja had turned south on Cat City Road, which passed Maytubby Springs on its way south. Maytubby told Renaldo what turns to make, and the cruisers were gaining ground as long as they stayed on dirt roads. But on State 22, where the Ninja veered west, the playing field was no longer even. The Cessna couldn't keep pace with the bike, either, but the Cessna was way up in the middle of the air.

At State 78, the bike turned north toward Milburn. The trooper and the deputy were two miles behind. Maytubby speed-dialed the Johnston sheriff's office and told the dispatcher to get a deputy to the First Baptist Church, where Jill was conducting her meeting. Not until he had ended the call did Maytubby summon to mind the biker's digital reserves. He already knew Jill's address and the date of her engagement to Maytubby, published in the *Ada News* along with her photo. He had seen her Accord on King's Road. The Chickasaw Nation's website had advertised the time and place of her meeting in Milburn.

He scrolled to Jill's name and called her. In a few seconds, he got her voice mail. She had good meeting manners. He called her again, knowing that it would do no good. A call from Hannah appeared on his phone screen. He ignored it. The green Ninja was minutes away. Renaldo and Katz had turned onto 78. He phoned Renaldo and told him the biker was going after Jill at the First Baptist Church. When he hung up, he mentally cataloged Jill's colleagues in the nation until he came to one who might know someone else at the meeting. The Ninja passed through Emet. Two short calls later, he was ringing the vice principal of Milburn High School. Not his first choice, but he was begging. How the vice principals of America must have cursed the invention of voice mail. Three rings, five, ten. Nothing.

Maytubby had an angle on the Ninja, but not enough of one to beat it to Milburn. He cut the throttle and dropped the plane's nose. He had to get down fast. The Ninja slowed to take a left turn into the little town. That bought Maytubby a few seconds to scout the streets leading into town. His flight instructor cut the power once during each lesson and said, "Land the plane." When they were fifty feet above the ground, the instructor throttled up and said only "You're alive" or "You're dead." More often than not, he was dead.

The Cessna's altimeter spun lefty. The highway through town was wide, its parallel parking deserted. Two power lines, near the central intersection, crossed the highway. The Ninja slewed into the church's lot, raising a gray cloud from the chat. Maytubby aimed for the very end of the highway curve so he could limbo under the lines. He set full flaps and slowed the plane, switched on the landing light. Out his left window, he saw the strobes of the cruisers. And ahead, coming toward him on 78, an ambulance.

He flashed the landing light just before his wheels yelped on the asphalt. The ambulance careened into a superette parking lot. His airspeed fell quickly into the forties, and he taxied on the quick march onto a lawn across from the church, behind a stand of bois d'arc trees, stomped the brakes, and cut the prop. The ambulance continued east. As the Continental sputtered to a stop, Maytubby grabbed his pistol and set off at a dead barefoot run toward the sheet-metal church.

He was not ten yards from the door when the cyclist, in a sand camo jumpsuit and matching helmet, visor up, burst into the lot, holding Jill by the hair. He pushed a long pistol against her ear.

"You stand down, Injun. I'll shoot your nigger whore. Drop that fucking pistol."

Maytubby let the gun fall on the chat. Jill stared at the ground and frowned diabolically, eyes wide open. Matted yellow hair fell across the biker's forehead. His eyes were large and feline chartreuse, his features small. The Ninja, idling, was pointed east, the way he had come.

The cruisers squealed into the lot. Renaldo and Katz drew their firearms and crouched behind their cruiser doors. "No!" Maytubby shouted. They saw the biker, holstered their guns, and stood with their hands atop the doors. The biker grabbed Jill's belt with his free hand, lifted her from the ground, and shoved her facedown onto the bike. He held the gun to her nape and mounted behind her. "If you follow me or set up a block, I will spill her brains all over your nice state highway." In a brisk turn, he holstered the pistol and sent a spray of gravel over the officers. The bike keened away.

In the brutal heat, Maytubby grew cold. As the white dust settled, he stood still, studying a mental map of the nation he had policed for three years. He scarcely noticed the arrival of a Johnston County deputy from the west, or the distraught members of Jill's committee huddling at the door of the church.

His reverie was broken by a jacked-up truck screeching around the 48 bend just as the cycle was leaving Milburn and making the curve south. Blue smoke rose from the truck's huge tires as it spun a 180 in the road. A body in its bed went overboard and rolled on the shoulder. It was a large body. Maytubby pointed down the road and shouted to Katz, "Get Deputy Bond and bring her to the plane!" Katz jumped into his cruiser and fetched her.

She swayed out of his cruiser, her uniform torn, knees and elbows bleeding.

"We're in the plane." Maytubby pointed. He turned to Renaldo, Katz, and the other Johnston County deputy. "Get down to Twenty-Two and Fort McCulloch Road. No strobes or sirens. And take Bee Emet Road, not Twenty-Eight. Keep your cells on."

Hannah Bond was fastening her lap belt when Maytubby climbed into the cockpit. "Katz told me about Jill. We'll get her back."

"Yes, we will."

"I gave that EMT pretty good directions," she said. "I would send a deputy to help him …"

"But the deputy who came is Eph."

"Yep."

"Clear the prop! Is Trepanier still alive?"

"Probably. Love was not going to quit until he found out who put him in Pontotoc. I heard that coming up on the house. When I busted in, he was out the door. So cranked he didn't see me grab his bumper. Drug me a ways before I got up in the bed."

Maytubby applied the left brake and pivoted the plane east. A small crowd had gathered in the superette lot, and some people were taking pictures with their phones. "How'd Love know to go there?"

"I saw cooking stuff. Trepanier might have gone there because one man he was running from didn't know about it."

Maytubby taxied onto the highway and pushed the throttle knob all the way in. He lifted off to the west and soon banked southeast.

"I have a name for the Ninja."

Maytubby looked at her.

"Hillers."

"I've got to keep my distance, but the glasses are good." Bond picked them up, focused them, and found the Ninja, just then turning east on State 22 and south on 78.

"Love's losing ground, but not as much as you'd think," Bond said.

Maytubby handed her his cell. "It's under 'Jake.'"

Bond told Renaldo what the Ninja was up to.

"He's going to make a mistake," Maytubbby said.

Bond leaned over Maytubby and pressed the glasses against her face. "He's turning east on …"

NAIL'S CROSSING · 191

"Prairie View Road. It turns into …"

"Nail's Crossing Road."

"Which doesn't cross the Blue like the wagons did."

"It's a dirt road, too, so everybody can see where he's going."

"Two mistakes. Who do you know with a car on Albert Pike Road?"

She raised her index finger and traced an imaginary Pike Road in the air, pausing at each imaginary house and mumbling the name of its owner. "Tic Miller," she said aloud. "Where Colonel Phillips Road meets it." Then she told Renaldo where the Ninja turned.

Maytubby cut the throttle and shortly added flaps. There were big power lines on the right side of Pike, and he had to get past a row of windbreak trees on the left so he could hug the ditch lip on that side. The plane floated just above the road as he coaxed the nose up inches at a time until the lift died and the wheels bumped down. Well below stall speed, he fed the old carburetor, and they moved briskly down the asphalt. "The Millers have any horses near the drive could get spooked?" Maytubby said.

"No horses, period. You stay in the plane while I ask Tic about the car." She looked at his bare feet on the rudder pedals. "You don't look official." She was wearing her police clothes.

He nodded. The driveway was not long, and at the margins was a large open space with a few rusted implements. An elderly man in denim overalls was on the porch before Maytubby killed the engine. Hannah strode quickly across the burned Bermuda grass, ignoring a snarling border collie that lunged at her boots. She did not talk to Miller long before his head bobbed and he fished in his pocket for keys.

Hannah opened the large doors of an old detached frame garage, once painted red, and disappeared inside. Taillights glowed, and a 1955 Chevy Task Force pickup with dung-spattered stock racks backed out fast. Maytubby grabbed his duty belt and water bottle. While Hannah Bond flicked the big floor shifter like a toothpick, getting the most bang out of the big six, Maytubby drank enough water and handed the bottle across the seat. Bond waved it away. He buckled on his duty belt and wiped his face with his T-shirt. Just as he put the glasses to his eyes, the Ninja, spawning a volcanic plume of gray dust, shot across Pike Road going east, on its way toward the rugged margins of the Blue.

Maytubby found Love's dust storm less than a mile west of Pike. The cell piped up. Renaldo told Maytubby he and Katz were crossing the river on foot above them and coming down the east bank. They would wait on Nail's Crossing Road.

"Hillers knows Love's truck, but Jill doesn't necessarily buy him anything with Love," Maytubby said. "Love doesn't know this truck. Let's fall in behind Love, but slowly. Is Love armed?"

"Yeah. He beat the Cajun with his fists, but he took a Remington Mountain Rifle out of that shanty."

"Scope?"

"No."

"Then not worth taking it from him now, except he might hit Jill with a junk shot."

The dust from the Ninja subsided. Love's did not. Hannah took off her campaign hat and unbuttoned her uniform top. Maytubby snatched Miller's beaten straw Western hat from the floorboard and put it on. He yanked Hannah's top down her back and threw it on the floorboard. Underneath, she was wearing a red Tishomingo Indians T-shirt paisleyed with sweat. They both removed their duty belts and stuck their pistols in their pants.

"I haven't been down this road in a while," Maytubby said under the glasses. Anybody live in that last building before the woods? The native stone?"

"Not since I've been working. Kids drink and fool around in there."

"Love's getting close. He's parking his truck across the road to block it."

Bond pulled into the driveway of the stone house. Out her passenger window, Maytubby watched Love through the glasses until the house eclipsed his view. Love, who was maybe fifty yards away, had pointed the rifle through his passenger window. He was staying with his truck in case he had to follow Hillers. In the turnaround, maybe forty yards beyond Love, the green Ninja circled as it had done on King's Road.

Bond killed the Chevy.

"I'm going, Hannah." He handed her the glasses.

Behind the house he found a rusted garden cultivator and wheeled it down an imaginary furrow, like a yeoman farmer, across a little clearing. By the time he reached cover and ditched the tool, he could hear Love shouting from his pickup, hoarse as a crow.

Maytubby ran fast. His farmer's hat peeled away.

"I already killed your preacher boy," Love shouted. "Not before he give you up." The Ninja circled faster. "Now I'm gonna kill *you.*"

Hillers juiced the Ninja a half second before the boom of the big rifle. Maytubby heard the *thock* of the slug hitting a bois d'arc trunk. The Ninja spun and retraced its ground, Hillers' smoked visor pivoting. The Remington's bolt clicked as Love ejected a casing. There was no way out for Hillers but the road Love blocked.

Maytubby stopped and crouched behind a red cedar. He wiped sweat from his eyes. Jill's black hair obscured her face, but he saw she had thrown her left arm over her neck. She was still. Hillers would dodge Love's next shot and then return fire. The Ninja leaped again, just before the boom echoed among the riverside outcrops. Maytubby heard splashing in the river behind him.

Hillers dismounted, drew his long pistol, and knelt. Maytubby sprinted for the motorcycle. Before the third report of Hillers' semiautomatic, Maytubby had Jill off the Ninja and was lying on top of her. He pulled his pistol from his belt and rolled, back-to-back with Jill. Hillers jumped to his feet and spun around. His visor did not nod to find them. Before Maytubby could find his mark, two pistol shots came from the woods behind him. A chunk of the motorcycle helmet burst away.

The shots continued as Hillers dropped his pistol and mounted the bike. It keened through the turnaround and up the road. He slowed at Love's truck, slid for a second into the bar ditch, and then got a purchase on the straight section road beyond.

But a new obstacle blocked Nail's Crossing Road: a filthy rusted truck from the middle of the last century, squatting sideways from ditch to ditch. Hillers braked and aimed for the shallower bar ditch to his left. As he was bracing for its lip, he looked up at a very large form in a sweaty red T-shirt.

*　*　*

Hannah Bond, first marksman in her CLEET graduating class, raised her much-ridiculed Smith Model 10 .357 Magnum in both hands, led the motorcycle by three feet, fired, and followed through. The Ninja pitchpoled, catapulting Hillers into a barbed-wire fence.

She ran up the road, came even with him, and fell prone in the sand. He was fighting the wire. She saw blood on his thigh. "Be still," she said.

His movements slowed but grew more methodical as he stripped the wire from his torso and legs.

"I said be still."

"Fuck you and the horse you rode in on," he said, limping free of the wire. She could see the house and road and herself mirrored in his visor. He lurched and rasped like the vulture that had ravaged one of his earlier kills.

Maytubby's words came back to her. The vulture was unarmed. She aimed at his heart but did not shoot.

He fell bleeding in the dust.

CHAPTER 30

Rotor beats from a Norman Regional medevac chopper turned heads at Nail's Crossing. The sky behind the craft took everyone by surprise: a bank of gray clouds—clouds that were not wildfire smoke.

Hannah Bond turned back to the task at hand, knotting a bandanna that, wound around the Model 10's barrel, would stanch the blood from Hillers' femoral artery. The bar ditch where she knelt was damp with blood. She didn't know if she had gotten the tourniquet on in time. Renaldo and Katz, their uniforms soaked from the waist down, stared at themselves in Hillers' visor.

* * *

In the shadow of the rock house, Jill threw back her head and guzzled hot water from Maytubby's bottle. He held a bloody compress of leaves under her nose as she drank. A violet bruise was spreading under her eyes and over her nose. After handing back the bottle, she held his shoulder for balance as she pulled a goathead from her heel. She had lost both shoes but refused to let Maytubby carry her to the car, because he had cut his instep on a broken beer bottle.

"His name is Hillers," Maytubby said.

She nodded and looked at the ground.

"He break your nose or did I?"

She looked toward Hillers and pointed with her chin.

As the chopper hovered over the road and began to settle, gray dust stung them all. They bowed their heads and covered their faces. When the dust had subsided, one of the EMTs confirmed that Love was dead. Katz volunteered to accompany Hillers in the medevac. The other EMT, while checking Hillers' vitals, told Hannah she would make a good field surgeon. She called an ambulance from Ada to retrieve Love's body and then drove Maytubby and Jill to the plane. In Miller's front yard, Hannah said, "I'll call Sheriff's Investigation in Tish."

"I'll call OSBI."

"They'll be tickled."

Maytubby taxied onto Albert Pike Road and was airborne in fifteen seconds. Banking west toward Ada, he and Jill looked at the squall line. "It seems otherworldly," she said.

"Computer generated."

"Yeah. I can't remember what rain is like."

The medevac chopper passed above them on its way to Norman.

He reached for her hand. They approached the darkening clouds in silence. Soon the crown of the storm obscured the sun. They flew in shadow the rest of the way. The sky opened as they were walking to the old Ford in Heartland Aviation's parking lot. They stopped and let the rain wash over them. They were soon joined by others at the airport—mechanics and clerks who spread their arms and turned their faces to the sky.

Maytubby slapped his portable Bull Blaster light-and-siren unit onto the roof of the pickup and plugged it into the cigarette lighter. As they hustled through downtown to the State 3 bypass, they got some odd looks. The whole ER staff of the Chickasaw Nation Medical Center, including the admissions clerk, crowded around Jill's exam bed. After a nurse closed the cubicle track curtains, Maytubby smiled at the scrub-pants millipede. He padded back to the waiting room in the pastel blue paper hospital slippers he was forced to wear when they came through the ER entrance. They had also given him a bandage for his foot.

As he unlocked his cell to call Scrooby, he saw a bulletin about the shooting on the waiting room television. Katz? Maytubby wondered. Hannah? His cell came to life, "OSBI" in the caller ID. Although he had been in the act of calling Scrooby just seconds before, now that Scrooby was calling him, he didn't feel like answering.

The phone was on its last ring before voice mail when he picked up. He stared out at the blue rain. "Dan."

"Bill. How far are you from Dove Road and State Seven?"

"Twenty minutes."

"Treepanty never came back, so our plain watched the Stoddard estate. Old Sol was apparently overcome by wanderlust. We just got a call from the Johnston sheriff to help with a murder investigation east of Milburn. I need to call the tail off for that."

Enough of the cat was out of the bag. "Austin Love is the Milburn victim. He found Trepanier and beat the name of the Ninja out of him. Hillers. Hillers kidnapped my fiancée, Jill Fox, drove her to Nail's Crossing on the Blue. Love chased him there. Hillers killed Love and tried to escape. OHP Renaldo and Deputy Katz crossed the Blue on foot and pursued. Hannah Bond blocked Nail's Crossing Road and shot him off his bike. Norman Regional coptered him out. Jill is okay. I'm here at the Chickasaw Nation Medical Center with her. I'm on my way to Dove Road. Address?"

For once, Scrooby did not blow. "Rough," he said. "I'll call Magaw in Tishomingo and ask to use his interrogation room. Stoddard will want counsel from the city. Love was a member of the Chickasaw Nation, so I'll call the FBI. I may have to stay the night in Tish. One-four-eight-six-two-five Dove Road. I know you don't have to write it down. If the Skywagon is free and we have a pilot, I'll be in Tish pretty soon. If not, two hours."

Maytubby jogged on his paper soles down the corridor to the

cubicle curtain and yanked it back. The bedside assembly stared at him. He said to Jill, "A certain pol is holed up south of Connerville. I'm going down there to watch him for OSBI."

Jill nodded from her bed, and he pulled the curtain shut.

When he was almost to his pickup, his cell rang. The ID said it was Heartland Aviation. "Maytubby."

"You do have pants on."

"Yeah, Frank. I had to get my fiancée to the ER."

"So you took your shirt and shoes off?"

"Long story. I'm on my way to get the gear." He looked down at his blue slippers. Addled. Good thing Frank called.

CHAPTER 31

When he turned off State 7 onto Dove Road, Maytubby used the police set in his pickup to radio Stoddard's tail. He described his pickup to the agent, who was so well concealed, Maytubby saw the address on a well-painted mailbox before he saw the tail. The drive winding off behind the mailbox was paved with discarded asphalt shingles laid in perfect rows as they would be on a roof. The tail's lights flashed up the road, and Maytubby pulled alongside the plain wrapper, which had been parked behind a blackberry patch inside a curve in the road.

"White Lexus ES?" Maytubby said. He didn't recognize the agent—a very young man, younger than Maytubby, with a shaved head.

"Yeah."

"Milburn is going to be a learning experience."

"You there?"

"Yes. You're going to need Mercator to map that crime scene."

"What?"

"Famous cartographer."

The agent shook his head.

"Mapmaker."

"Oh. Okay." A little smirk crept into the agent's face. "See you." He drove away.

Maytubby parked behind the blackberry bushes, which were shiny from the rain. He reached out of the cab and picked a few berries from a stem and ate them while he Googled Stoddard's old House race donor list and the Dove Road address. Evelyn Hunter. The name meant nothing to him. He paired it with Stoddard's in a Google search. The only useful hit was the donor list he had already seen.

Afternoon sun gilded the towering thunderheads moving eastward. Mansions of nothingness. A phrase from a poem Maytubby partly remembered. The rain would feel good to Hannah and Jake, but it would make a pig's breakfast of the bald agent's crime scene.

The rain had brought up mosquitoes from Tar Branch. It was still too hot to roll up the truck's windows, so Maytubby waved and swatted at them. Less than an hour later, he saw OSBI's big workhorse Cessna descending toward Tishomingo.

Fifteen minutes later, Magaw's cruiser, with Scrooby riding shotgun, trundled down Dove Road. Magaw parked behind the pickup. All three men stood in the steamy afternoon.

Magaw shook his head. "Hannah called me from Milburn," he said to Maytubby. "You and her couldn't keep out of it." He looked at Scrooby. Scrooby looked into the distance. "Hannah was lucky she wasn't shot in that nonsense."

"Hannah Bond would not be a person I'd say is in need of luck," Maytubby said softly. "The thug who killed Majesty Tate—that fellow with the really fast motorcycle and the thousand-dollar pistol? The one Hannah shot on the fly? That guy was in need of luck. He must've had some, though, or she would've shot his balls off."

Magaw spat at a fencepost. "Scrooby, you and the tribal policeman can talk to Mr. Stoddard. No use in a crowd."

Scrooby and Maytubby walked slowly up the shingled drive. At the end, they found a blonde-brick ranch with forest-green cast-iron porch posts. The matching trim had recently been painted. Three holly shrubs, poodle-trimmed, grew on each side of the porch. The Lexus was parked next to the house.

Scrooby rang the doorbell, which played "Für Elise." Scrooby looked at Maytubby. "Beethoven," Maytubby said.

A middle-aged woman with a silver bob opened the door. She was wearing a magenta wool suit and black pumps. A gust of camphor spilled onto the small concrete porch. Behind her, they could see a blue satin couch with crocheted doilies on the arms. And a pistol lying on an end table. The woman frowned severely. "Yes?"

Scrooby held out his badge and identified himself and Maytubby. "We would like to speak with Solomon Stoddard."

She grew erect and said loudly, "And what is the nature of your request to speak with Mr. Stoddard?"

"We need to speak with him in private, ma'am."

If it were possible, she stiffened even more. "I'm certain Mr. Stoddard has no need to answer questions from officers of the law. You are well aware that he is a champion of all law enforcement agencies and has, in his years in the state legislature, voted generous funding for them."

"Yes ma'am, I am," Scrooby said. "He helped me get a raise. Could you please ask him to step out here?"

The Lexus ignition was quiet but not silent. The car shot backward down the drive, slewed at a wide spot, then spun its front wheels, spinning up shingles like Frisbees. Scrooby and Maytubby gave chase. The OSBI agent was surprisingly quick. At the first curve of the driveway, they could see the Lexus' brake lights—and Magaw's cruiser, blocking Stoddard at the county road. Magaw was leaning against his car, legs crossed, sucking a toothpick.

Stoddard got out of the Lexus, his face red, the veins in his forehead bulging. He was wearing a buff linen suit and a red sport shirt. The shirt was darkened by perspiration. "What the hell is all this!" he sputtered.

Scrooby panted as he approached Stoddard. "We want to talk to you about the murder of Majesty Tate."

Stoddard rolled his eyes. "Oh, yeah. Got it. I run for high office, here come the jackals. Okay. Where's your warrant?"

Scrooby said, "At this time, we only—"

"Johnston County DA's talking to the judge right now," Magaw drawled. "Half hour at the most."

"On what grounds …?"

Maytubby stepped up to him.

"An *Indian* cop? You've got to be kidding. You have no juris—"

"No sir, I don't. Sheriff Magaw and agent Scrooby here are in charge. But I have been assisting them since the first suspect in the murder of Majesty Tate—a member of the Chickasaw Nation—was exculpated."

"What?"

"The Indian didn't kill her."

"So?"

Maytubby continued quietly, "Your creature Basile Trepanier—the guy you got off with the pro bono champagne defense—knew a hired gun named Hillers who would dispose of a lovely young prostitute named Majesty Tate. She posed a threat to your campaign. Hillers forced Trepanier to find a fall guy. Trepanier, while he was guiding his flock at Sun Ray Gospel Fellowship, infiltrated a meth ring in Antlers and found an ex-con named Austin Love whom he could throw together with Majesty Tate after she had learned you were running for governor and after she had left the city."

"Bullshit, bullshit, and bull*shit!*" Stoddard stamped his foot.

"Hillers waited until Love and Tate had been together; then he butchered her …"

Stoddard's eyes flinched.

"… with a Bowie knife identical to Love's. After he left the Pontotoc jail, Love found Trepanier and beat Hillers' name out of him. A few hours ago, Hillers shot Love to death at Nail's Crossing on the Blue. Sheriff Magaw's deputy"—Maytubby nodded toward Magaw—"Hannah Bond, shot Hillers off his motorcycle. He was flown to Norman Regional. Trepanier was taken by ambulance to Mercy Hospital in Tishomingo."

Stoddard stood as rigid as his Puritan namesake. A distant siren wailed on US 377.

"Hillers also kidnapped and assaulted my fiancée. She may not live."

"Sol? Sol?" A quavering voice grew louder behind them. Evelyn Hunter stumbled across her shingles. She stopped when she saw the officers. Then she turned and walked away.

The cruiser bumped up Dove Road, its siren blaring and strobes pulsing. When it came to a stop, Maytubby recognized Eph.

"Turn that shit off!" Magaw said. Eph ducked back in the cruiser and did as he was told. Then he carried an envelope to Magaw. With great ceremony, the sheriff opened the envelope, pulled out its contents, and read, "Solomon Stoddard, you are under arrest for the charge of conspiracy to commit murder." He then handcuffed Stoddard and led him to his own patrol car.

"I seen him on TV," Eph said. "He's a coach or somethin'."

When the county cars had left, Scrooby turned to Maytubby. "She may not live?"

Maytubby shrugged.

CHAPTER 32

"I have something to tell you," Jill said. She was lying on the couch in her garage apartment, wearing a peach knit shirt and buff boxers. Maytubby, still in his Lighthorse uniform, unwrapped chicken shawarma, hummus, and pita takeout from Mazen's. He put them on plates on her coffee table. "That smells delicious," she said.

"How is your nose?"

"My great-grandfather lived in this apartment when he was the chauffeur for the oilman in the big house."

Maytubby held a dripping swatch of foil above the food.

"You told me once that his father was a freedman."

"Not that you needed to be told." She pointed to her face. "His son married a woman who was half Chickasaw. In those days, the nation, you know, had been adjudicated almost out of existence."

"And the descendants of freedmen were still on shaky ground."

"Still are, in some precincts of the so-called civilized tribes."

Maytubby balled up the foil and threw it away. He brought forks and knives from the kitchen. "One of the reasons they were called 'civilized': they owned slaves."

They ate in silence

"What did your great-grandfather drive for the oilman?"

She wiped hummus from her lips. "You man. All I can say is, it was a big car. How did you cut your foot?"

Maytubby looked at the bandage the CNHC PA had bound his foot with after suturing it. "I ain't sayin'."

"Choc bottle."

"Not Choc."

"How do you know?"

"Give me your dish. I'll wash up."

"Is Hillers alive?"

"Yes. He made a mess of the Norman Regional ER. Katz had to subdue him. FBI's in charge of him now."

"Trepanier?"

"Severe concussion. Broken clavicle. Induced coma. They'll take him to the OU Medical Center Hospital in the next couple of days."

"And keep him away from Hillers."

"Yes." Maytubby took a bag of frozen peas from Jill's tiny freezer and laid it gently on her face, then washed the dishes and stacked them in the drainer. He looked out over the universe of sodium lamps, little galaxies at Kerr Lab and CNMC and Ahloso. Then he limped to the couch, where Jill pulled up her legs and made room for him. She had bandages on both knees.

"Scrooby came around on old Sol pretty quick in the end."

"I think he came around a while before he let on."

"Think he was exasperated with himself?"

Maytubby smiled. He stared at her bruises. "You look like a coon."

"You're the second person today who's told me that."

"Think your great-great-grandmother was from the Raccoon clan?"

"I'm told she was proud, so maybe. I have something for you. Turn around and reach down to the floor."

Maytubby flipped on the couch and groped in the shadows. He pulled up a new felt campaign hat.

"Brought to you by US Police Supply and FedEx."

He donned it and preened. "I owe you a new pair of panty hose."

"Yes, you do, Sergeant. But they will have the opposite effect."

"After today, do you long for Brooklyn and the Texarkana fire-eater?"

"Not for a second. What I do long for is sleep."

"You want to have breakfast with Hannah day after tomorrow?"

"Yes. Can you put these peas back in the freezer?"

When he returned, Jill was asleep. He turned off the lights and lay on the opposite end of the couch. He took off the hat and laid it on the floor. In seconds, he was asleep.

Sometime in the night, a motorcycle roared down Broadway. They both sat up on the couch.

"He's in restraints," Jill said. The sound receded.

"Yuh," he said as they both fell back.

At nine the next morning, both their cells came alive. Again at ten and eleven. They slept until dusk.

CHAPTER 33

The day after that, Maytubby had officially been AWOL for a day. When Sheila buzzed him into Lighthorse HQ, he had driven from his own house, where he had enjoyed another long sleep. His cell showed twenty-six missed calls and ten messages. "How's Jill?" she asked him.

"She has two big shiners. She's at work today."

"Have you seen the TV coverage?"

"I don't have a television." "You landed a plane on Pike Road?"

"A very small plane."

"Did you hurt your foot?"

"Stepped on some glass."

"You should always wear shoes."

"So I've been told."

Les Fox looked up at Maytubby through the plate glass of his office. Maytubby walked on to his desk, which was again littered with sticky notes. He heard Fox's tread on the carpet and quickly picked up his desk phone. Not fast enough.

Fox stood in his doorway, his legs spread and his arms across his chest. "Out of the blue of the western sky."

Maytubby put the phone back in its cradle. "Uh …"

"*Sky King.* You know."

"Sorry."

"Kirby Grant, fifties TV drama about an Arizona rancher who chases rustlers and such in his plane."

Maytubby shook his head.

"You're too young. One of those messages"—he pointed to the desk—"is from a *New York Times* stringer."

"He should interview Hannah Bond."

"Hannah Bond is an Anglo county deputy. Zero exotic Indian interest."

Maytubby stared hard. "You know that Jill Milton is my fiancée."

Fox gripped his forearms tighter.

Maytubby said, "You know Hillers tried to take me out in McCurtain."

"You were freelancing …" Fox frowned and let his arms drop and put his hands in his pockets. "But yeah." He looked at the ceiling and exhaled. "You were never a showboater. You pay for the plane yourself?"

"Yes."

"Give me a receipt, and the nation will reimburse you." He walked away.

Maytubby called every press number and said to everyone who answered, "I have no comment." Then he called Scrooby.

"Stoddard's counsel won't let him talk. The trophy wife has filed for divorce. Hillers' DNA is a match for the Tate murder and two Arkansas murders."

"Did …?"

"Yes. I called Detective Washington. He can close. Treepanty is still in a coma. Hillers has a PD but won't talk to anyone. Just glares at the ceiling. Katz says he's a scary mother."

"Phoo-*oo,* he's a scary mother!"

Scrooby chuckled. "Exactly. Later."

CHAPTER 34

Hannah Bond, wearing her full Johnston County deputy uniform, was already seated at a table in JD's Café in Ada when Maytubby and Jill walked in at 7:00 a.m. It was a dimly lit place with red drapery blocking the windows, and lattice screens between the tables and an empty lunch buffet. Hannah was studying the menu. She looked up and nodded sheepishly.

Jill tucked into her seat, Maytubby sitting next to her. There were menus on the table. Jill picked hers up, scanned it quickly, and said, "My grandfather was a hand at calf fries. I'm going to order that and scrambled eggs and home fries and biscuits with gravy."

Hannah turned questioning eyes on Maytubby. He ignored her and studied the menu. "I think I'm going for oatmeal and prunes."

Jill and Hannah looked at each other. "Prunes," Hannah said.

ACKNOWLEDGMENTS

I am deeply indebted to my gifted editor, Michael J. Carr, whose skill, cheer, and advocacy went above and beyond.

Jason O'Neill, former Chickasaw Lighthorse chief of police, patiently explained the basics of tribal jurisdiction. Any errors on this score are mine and not his.

My dear friends Sarah Miracle and Jill Fox read the manuscript and supplied details about nutrition education. Neva Harjochee provided some vital cultural nuance. Jason Eyachabbe introduced me to the Chickasaw language and corrected Chickasaw dialogue in the story. Cody Dixon was a thorough guide on our tour of the Kullihoma Grounds.

Warm thanks to those who commented on the manuscript and answered my pesty questions: Karleene Smith, Susan Lackey Parker, Young Smith, Desiree Hupy, Jim Rosenthal, Amanda Boyden, Wendy Jones, Jeff Buckles, Stuart Stelly, Kim Oliver, Joan Schoenfeld, Reggie Poche, Dale Wares, Paul Swenson, Rocky Robbins.

A hearty salute to Jenny, the owner of Norman's Gray Owl Coffee, and to the shop's crew of brilliant baristas, who daily solved vocabulary and diction puzzles: Laney, Laura, Andrew, Rachel, Chris, Roshni, Jasmine, Erika. A shout-out to Rob at Michelangelo's Coffee.

Many thanks to my agent, Richard Curtis.

A Q&A WITH
KRIS LACKEY

Q: Was there a particular event, idea, or image that inspired you to write *Nail's Crossing*?

A: On a visit to Ada in 2011, I saw a Lighthorse Police cruiser. The term "lighthorse" is a survival from Indian Territory days. It distinguishes a small mounted force from the cavalry. That cruiser fetched my imagination.

Q: What is your connection to the Chickasaw Nation?

A: I am an Anglo, with no indigenous heritage. The first time I was aware of the Chickasaw Nation was when I studied Oklahoma history in junior high school. My elderly teacher, in the 1960s, described Indian removal with sympathy rare for the times. I wrote a report in high school on the Civil War in Indian Territory and learned that some of the removed nations held slaves and took sides in the conflict.

Q: The landscape is described so vividly in the book. What kind of research did you do to capture the setting?

A: In preparation for *Nail's Crossing* I read books about the Chickasaws, interviewed members of the nation, took an introductory language class, and haunted the library of the Oklahoma Historical Society. To get the lay of the land I drove lots of country roads in my tiny hybrid. I have worn out three copies of the *Oklahoma Atlas and Gazetteer*.

Q: How would you describe the dynamic between Maytubby and Bond?

A: They trained together and finished at the top of their CLEET class. They are tight friends, easy with ribbing each other. They negotiate their cultural differences with humor and respect.

Q: Is there a particular time of day you prefer to dedicate to writing?

A: Brief stints: late morning and late afternoon.

Q: Do you have any writing rituals?

A: I write in coffee shops. The bustle and white noise keep me alert and focused. And I have many diction questions for the baristas.

Q: Did you outline before you wrote the book, or was your approach less structured?

A: The detectives and I are on the same page. I am as baffled as they are.

Q: Your writing style has been called "unusual," "unique," "flavorful," and "different but effective." What do you think readers mean by this?

A: I don't know. Whet the knife, pare and pare. That's all I do. An old biographer once told me, "Never underestimate your reader's intelligence." So when I think the reader can go it alone, I don't explain. Action and dialogue should do the heavy lifting. I don't like to meddle.

Q: If you were to create the soundtrack for *Nail's Crossing* the movie, which particular songs or musicians would you include to help tell the story?

A: Two soundtracks: Neil Young's work on Jim Jarmusch's film *Dead Man*; Explosion in the Sky's music for the film *Friday Night Lights*. I also like the dark takes on Texas swing by Café Noir.

Q: Your previous book was a work of nonfiction, *RoadFrames: The American Highway Narrative*, which Douglas Brinkley praised as "without a doubt...the finest interpretive analysis of US highway literature ever written." Readers have remarked that in the scenes in *Nail's Crossing* when Maytubby is in his patrol car on the highway, they feel like they are right in the car with him. Do you think your in-depth knowledge of on-the-road literature helped to bring these scenes to life?

A: A prevailing fantasy of nonfiction road writers is that they are reexperiencing the "virgin gaze" of the European explorer. Maytubby knows too much history to fall into this trap. He knows, for instance, that plains tribes roamed his landscape before the Chickasaws arrived. But when he returns to a place like Boggy Depot, he connects it to the specific privations of his ancestors. He and Jill Milton also understand the circumstances of the enslaved victims of removal. They cannot share the romantic road vision of Anglo travelers.

Q: Who are the authors, critics, poets, musicians, or artists you admire?

A: That's a lot to bite off. Shakespeare, Cervantes, Samuel Johnson, George Eliot, Tolstoy, Gogol, Turgenev, on and on. Classic American fiction writers: Melville, Wharton, James, Faulkner, Cather, Hemingway, Baldwin, Ellison, Larsen, Fitzgerald. Modern fiction writers: Marilynne Robinson, Charles Portis, Cormac McCarthy, Sherman Alexie, Toni Morrison, Edward St. Aubyn, Kent Haruf, Larry McMurtry. I love *The Book of Ebenezer Le Page* by G. B. Edwards and *The Colony of Unrequited Dreams* by Wayne Johnston. They are essentially frontier writers. Poets: my American squeezes are Dickinson, Frost, and Billy Collins.

Q: Who are your favorite mystery writers?

A: I admired Tony Hillerman's Navajo mysteries long ago. Hillerman was an Oklahoma native. I met and talked with him when I worked at the University of New Mexico. Gentle man, good listener. His detectives, Jim Chee and Joe Leaphorn, are calm men with a good sense of humor. I also like the Dave Brandstetter series by Joseph Hansen and K. C. Constantine's Mario Balzic crime novels. Georges Simenon's thrift and eye for telling detail stick with me.

Q: What about giving any spoilers away ... What can readers expect from the next Maytubby/Bond adventure?

A: Maytubby and Bond investigate the apparently random murders of two upstanding citizens. The detectives tail a smuggling ring camouflaged by a vending-machine business.

Q: Is there a particular question that you wish an interviewer would ask you? What would your answer be?

A: What is your granddaughter's newest word? "Elbow."